They Call It Treason

ISBN **978-1-947514-33-1**

Printed in the United States of America

St. Clair Publications
P. O. Box 726
Mc Minnville, TN 37111 – 0726

http://stclairpublications.com

Cover drawing, "John Leans Down," adapted, Logopit, Woman's History Museum;
colorization, Michele Prater Walker

Cover design, by Kent Hesselbein

KGB Design Studio
Manchester, TN, USA

http://kghdesign.nvaazion.com/

Other historical works by Stanley J. St. Clair include:

A Proud Heritage: The James Ansel Vinson Family Story; Maternal Family History, 1999, St. Clair Publications limited printing, OOP

Still available:

Prayers of Prophets, Knights and Kings; History of Prayer, 2006, Trafford Publishing Co.

Mysterious People of the Bible in the Light of History; 2008, St. Clair Publications

A Place in Time; Reconstruction Era Novella, 2009, St. Clair Publications

Conspiracy in the Town that Time Forgot; True Crime Drama, 2009, St. Clair Publications

Quinn; Family Historic Novella based on a True Story, 2009, St. Clair Publications

Beyond the Thistle Patch; Memoirs of Youth, 2010, St. Clair Publications

Turning Point at Gettysburg; Civil War Historic Novel based on a True Story, 2021, St. Clair Publications

They Call it Treason

They Call It Treason

The Legend of Christiana Crewey

A Novel of
Colonial Virginia
and the American Revolution

Based on a True Story

Illustrated with Epilogue

Stanley J. St. Clair

Edited by Matthew Jackson

StCP

Introduction

A great deal of extensive research was done in an effort to make this story as historically accurate as possible. I have included a reference list in the back of this book of sources used. The main characters are real people and the major events actually happened. Dates within the family story were at times hazy and adjusted to make the plot flow well. Much of the actual lives of the characters are fictionalized.

When delving deep into our family history we often uncover facts of which are not proud, as it was for me with the betrayal and court martial of an ancestor; but they all fit together to make us who we are.

They Call it Treason is based on the true story of George and Christiana Crewey Walters, my fourth great grandparents. In my story, Christiana was born in Holland, and had studied very intently to obtain a good education in mid-eighteenth century England.

George was a ruggedly handsome young British brick mason, but uneducated and opinionated. Drawn in by his good looks, his hard work and sincere desire for a better life, Christiana married him and joined him on a voyage aboard what turned out to be a slave ship to the

Virginia Colony where they had been promised a land grant to grow tobacco for sale in England by the Virginia House of Burgesses. Taking up a large section of property on the cusp of the Great Eastern Divide, they started a family, which grew as they gradually reached for their goals.

When the American Revolution broke out, George was fiercely loyal to the Crown, King George III, the father of whom he saw as the source of all their good fortune. Being fairly forced to serve in the Revolutionary Virginia Militia, after only a brief time, he deserted and joined the regulars, the British military.

After being captured and spending two years in jail, he was court-martialed and compelled to serve eighteen months in the Continental Army under General George Washington.

Christiana, who was very pro American, was furious! She refused to own slaves. With a big family and a plantation to run, what would she do?

Her actions and family would make her a legend.

This book highlights the bravery and heroism of several legendary women in the early era of Colonial and Revolutionary America.

Expressions and spellings reflect time period.

Like my previous novel, *Turning Point at Gettysburg*, it is narrated by its main character.

Genealogy

George Walters – Christiana Crewey

George Anthony Walters – Mary Kirby

Henry C. Walters – Elizabeth Davis

Sallie Bell Walters – John Meddow St. Clair

Archie Morris St. Clair – Lula Gay Graham

Marvin Woodrow St. Clair – Trula G. Vinson

Stanley J. St. Clair

Chapter One

My name is Christiana Crewey Walters; well, it was, at least. We'll get to that later.

I have jotted down a lot of notes and saved quite a few newspaper articles during my lifetime in hopes that one day I might be able to preserve the most important details of my adventurous life story, and that of my family, for future generations.

I was born in rural Holland, near Amsterdam, in February 1730. There was some question about the exact day of my birth, but I have always celebrated on the 17th. My parents were strict Sabbath-keeping believers in the Holiness religion. They had their own fellowship separate from other churches when I was a wee lassie.

Some of Papa's ancestors were known as the "Black Dutch," a group of Africans who came to Amsterdam in the 17th century as soldiers, musicians, dancers, singers and servants.

According to my papa, Chrisyan Crewey, his grandfather, a local gardener, had married one of the servants. Because of this, my skin is slightly darker than most, but very little.

My great grandfather, Papa said, was working for a Portuguese Jewish family in Amsterdam. He became attracted to one of their domestic servants. According to Papa she had a lovely disposition and was very intelligent. She had learned to speak both Dutch and Portuguese, and told him fascinating stories about her tribal life in Africa. The family members where she worked had treated her very kindly and were delighted by their devotion to one another. They had been married by the Jewish Rabbi in their home.

My parents had gone through the Pachter-soproer riots around the time they got married. That's what they called the Dutch rebellion. Rural tax collection and the way the landed gentry handled their power had brought about much unrest.

I remember when I was a young girl, my papa having visions of future events. I recall well his telling me, "Christy, you'll someday be a goin' across the sea to th' New World and makin' somethin' o' yourself!"

Well, that's the meaning of what he said in Dutch, and the way someone like him would say it nowadays.

The wealth of our country was on a sharp decline when I was a child. I can't recall a lot from Holland because I was so young, but I remember the beauty and smell of the myriads of tulips, and the consistent turning of windmills about the countryside. They were a new thing then, but I hear they are increasing in number.

At my age six, Papa got a chance to move our family to England. We went on a small ship with a friend of Papa's from the church who had relatives in London. I had a younger brother and sister, and my mama was frail. I know he was hoping to give us younguns a chance at a better life, and maybe help his prophecy to be fulfilled.

Papa got us into school as soon as we could get settled in London. He was insistent on us being the best we could be—especially me, his firstborn and namesake. I didn't like the city, and conditions in our neighborhood were poor, to say the least, as were we.

Everyone could tell from his accent and ways of doing things that Papa was a butter-bag—that's what they called Dutchmen in London. But he learned enough English before we moved there to get a decent job as a doorman at a big hostel and saved every penny possible to make sure we got our education.

I gained knowledge of the English language quickly and became a top student within the first year. That's because I wanted it more than most of the British children. The school was closely linked to the Church of England, so I was taught rigid discipline. Because of my good grades and Papa's willingness to pay, I was able to enroll in a private secondary school after finishing free grammar school. Not only did I learn reading, writing and arithmetic, I learned some important skills in school. Of course Mama had taught me the basics of cooking, but I picked up a lot more in the secondary school and didn't forget how to apply it. I also was taught how to make nice-looking clothes from simple cotton cloth. Sewing was one of my favorite subjects, and it came in very handy in real life.

After graduation from the secondary school, at seventeen, I began work as a hostess in the hostel where Papa was employed.

This proved as good a job for me as I could get in that day and time in London. They even let me off on holy days. I was able to buy decent clothes and help support my younger brother and sister. The work there would also prove invaluable to me in later years.

I advanced to a management position within a year or so, and stayed so busy with my work and my family that I found no time for men. Of course I was still very young.

Though we didn't have much time to talk, I saw my papa at work, and I tried to go to see my mama as often as possible. She was thin and had a pale visage. I felt so sorry for her. I talked to some of the other girls I worked with and one of them told me that sometimes wearing a corset too tightly could cause a lady to be that way. I tried not to laugh out loud; though I'm quite sure I snickered. The girl didn't let on like she heard me though. My poor mother never owned a corset in her life! Mama couldn't afford to go to a doctor, and wouldn't have dared accept charity.

Then, in the spring of 1749, while working at the front desk, a short, rugged, yet handsome young fellow came in to get a room. I don't know what there was about him, but I felt a strange sensation when I first saw him. Obviously his dark complexion was from working outdoors, but his skin tone was a lot like mine.

His name was George Walters. He began a conversation with me, and told me that he was from the border region of England with Scotland. He had walked every step of the way from his home to London, camping along the road at night.

I knew from this, as well as from his dress and mannerism, that he was poor and uneducated; but I couldn't get him off my mind after he went to his room. He had registered to pay by the week, signing with an X.

He spoke to me cheerfully every morning as he left the hostel. One day after his first week had expired, he told me that he was working for a local builder as a brick mason and that he had an uncle in Lancaster, Pennsylvania. He was counting on a new start in America. I had not the slightest notion when or how he expected to accomplish this.

He asked me if I would be kind enough to have dinner with him that evening at the nearby tavern. I was a bit hesitant, as I had never taken up with any man, but agreed because I felt so strangely drawn to him.

That evening, at dinner, he asked about my family, and in the term of our talk, he told me that he had plans to journey to America in the near future. His uncle in Pennsylvania was to pay his fare. I already knew that a lot German people had also settled there. George's uncle, his Scottish mother's brother, had also emigrated from Scotland to that area and was talking of the possibility of obtaining lands in the Virginia Colony. Though I had no hold on George, my papa's words rang in my ears. "Someday you'll travel to the New World…"

George was very kind and considerate. He didn't try to kiss me or push himself on me in any way. He just told me that he enjoyed our time together and said goodnight. I was then nineteen and he, barely eighteen. He was so unusual for an eighteen-year-old. Very mature seeming. I felt flattered and honored to have caught the attention of this handsome young fellow.

That's how it all began.

Chapter Two

George was a steady, dependable worker and had no trouble keeping his job. He saved most of what he made, as the cost of his stay at the hostel was small. He and I became close friends and he began to respectfully court me on a regular basis within the first month after his arrival. He would tell me stories about his life up in the far North of England and his family. He told me that the land there had once been like a no man's land up until the 1600s. His papa's parents had moved there searching for a homestead and had become dirt farmers.

He never tried to make love to me, though I would likely have given in because it was obvious that I was falling in love with the handsome young bloke.

We began going out to see the sights of the city on the weekends when both of us had time off work, though neither of us owned a carriage, or even a horse. I especially enjoyed strolling through the Vauxhall Gardens, though it was plain to see that it was out of George's league and comprehension. He smiled and nodded when he didn't understand something I was talking about. He just seemed to want to please me at the time.

Yes, I certainly knew that George had little or no schooling, so I did my best not to use any break-teeth words around him.

Luckily, I was also frugal, and had accumulated a few pounds sterling. Of course a hostel wasn't the highest paying employer, due to low rates helping the needy, but my room and board were furnished. My needs were few after my brother and sister got older and went out on their own. Neither of them went past charity school, so they were in mediocre paying positions, but were able to support themselves in a meager lifestyle. Only a few young people in London were finding spouses early; the average was considerably older than we were. The poorer ones merely wanted to get married to improve their lives and settle down. Some were just eager to get away from deprived conditions at home.

My brother, Christopher, a year younger than I, now was a craftsman apprentice and had already wed. His wife, Emma, was his same age and had just discovered that she was expecting their first little one. They lived in a second-story three-room flat with simple wooden furniture. But they were happy.

My sister, Sophie, now sixteen, was working as a maid for a banker. She had a great personality and was loved by the family and given quarters in their home. She had told me that she was going to take her time when it came to marriage, as she had a fine life already.

Papa had been able to move into a smaller, two-room flat and required less money to survive.

Over taxation, I had quickly learned, was not confined to Holland. We were taxed heavily in England as well and I became resistant to George II. It made me wish that my beau's name was something different. I never mentioned it to him, though, because he had made no secret of the fact that he was proud of his Christian name, and the fact that it was the same as that of the King. Politics was obviously off limits for us.

The tavern, I had soon found out, belonged to the Thornhills, who also owned the hostel in which Papa and I were employed. At times, now, they shifted me to working as a hostess at the tavern. But I didn't mind, because the work was enjoyable, and not too taxing.

One evening while we were dining there, George gently took my hand, got down on one knee, and spoke tenderly to me while his steel grey eyes were gazing deep into my dark brown ones.

"Me dear darlin', Christy, ye know how methinks o' ya. I love ya and want ya ta spend yer life by me side! Will ya please do me th' honor o' becomin' me wife?"

I can't say that I didn't anticipate this, as he had always treated me with the greatest deal of respect and I felt his love.

"Yes, George, you handsome scoundrel! I'll marry you!" I blurted out, as a wide smile turned into a giggle. I was acting like a twelve-year-old. But I was also in love, or thought I was, and very much looked forward to having a family of my own.

That night he kissed me passionately, drawing me close to his muscular frame. I almost invited him into my room; but still being a virgin, I knew it proper to stay so until after our nuptials. Also, I knew that this would encourage a short engagement.

Over the next few days we moved quickly to set a date for our wedding. We were married in

Historic St. Giles Parish Church, which was in its third and as far as I know, present edifice, on Wednesday, 11 September 1749, at 6:00 in the evening. Since none of his relatives lived in London, the guests consisted only of my family members and our friends from the hostel, the tavern and his job. It was a lovely ceremony, for which my papa and I paid the sum total. The Thornhills put us up in the nicest suite they had, reserved for their visiting family members and dignitaries who were their friends. Come to think of it, it was the only suite besides the one occupied by the Thornhills, themselves.

**Hograth's *Noon*, from Four Times of the Day,
1738 Carving,
St. Giles Parish Church in the background**

We wasted no time starting our family, as we were Anglicans and believed that God sent us into the world to create more of our kind.

After only a few months I discerned that I was expecting, but both of us were anxious to journey to the New World. Two months earlier we had received the money from George's uncle for his passage, and I had enough from my savings to pay mine with more for our use in America.

George had passionate dreams of becoming a planter, and his uncle had told us in his last letter that the de facto Governor of the Virginia Colony, Thomas Lee, was now making land grants to serious immigrants wanting to grow tobacco for the Virginia House of Burgesses. At least in Pennsylvania he was able to get mail out to London by British Imperial Post. There were placards up all over Lancaster. We had sent a letter to Lee and had just received cordial communication asking us to meet with him at the Governor's Palace in Williamsburg as soon as we arrived in the colony.

A new life awaited. We were beside ourselves as we boarded the ship in Liverpool heading for Virginia.

Chapter Three

We were unaware when we boarded that the ship, the *Molly*, was carrying slaves which had been rounded up in Bristol, Africa. Some were being sold in England whilst the rest were headed to America. We were only told that it was the first available passage to the Virginia Colony. I felt ill and violated. Partly, I suppose, because of what I had learned about my own heritage.

Account sheet from the slave ship Molly

It was Monday, 2 March. There was not even a log of passengers since we were the only persons on the *Molly* who were not crew or enslaved Africans. I think the captain just put our money in his pocket and told no one that we were aboard. Now I understood why our fare was less than we expected. At least I couldn't be sorry for that part. Luckily, my pregnancy was still in the early stages and there was no danger of giving birth aboard the ship.

But we were on our way, and all we could do was accept our circumstances and sail on. By some miracle, George didn't get sea sick, but the combination of my condition, the stench rising from the bowels of the ship and the jiggling of the *Molly* on the high seas made me deathly ill.

George was kind and tried his very best to comfort me and remain close by my side. He would hold my hand and wrap his arm around me and tell me he loved me and that everything would be alright.

The mess worker brought our meals to our cabin, but at first the mere sight of food made me throw up and I had nothing but water on my stomach! What a miserable existence that was! I would feel a bit better in the evenings, and tried to eat. I could only take in so much though, and that, soft foods.

Thankfully there was only one bad storm on our voyage. We had been sailing for about three weeks when we were awakened in the wee hours of night by harsh claps of thunder incessantly rumbling. The sky would light up like mid-day then everything would go as dark as pitch. Sleep would come no more that night. The massive sails had to be skillfully lowered by the deck crew to keep the whipping seas from completely destroying them and possibly even our vessel. George stayed calm, laid close to me and held me in his muscular arms. Oh, if only that security could have continued to this day!

The storm only lasted one day and didn't throw us too much off course, but we were told that the correction and rerouting cost us several days.

It took us seven weeks and two days to reach Williamsburg, where George and I were permitted to disembark that evening before the *Molly* continued to the Potomac and up to Alexandria.

I thanked the Heavenly Father that we no longer had to be aboard that putrid ship!

It was Wednesday the 22nd of April and a puffy zephyr was blowing as we walked into that wonderful coastal town. Painted buckeyes and blue and white wild indigos were in bloom all around us. Colourful phlox graced the fronts of the lawns. As we continued to stroll along I began to spot large patches of breathtaking tulips! Red ones, orange ones, pale yellow and pink ones! Straight away my mind raced back to my innocent childhood in Holland! I could smell their fragrance wafting on the breeze! In that cryptic moment I sorely missed my precious mother.

Dusk was falling. We soon were able to find us a clean room for the night in an inn, and after a refreshing bath and hot breakfast the next morning, we made our way to the Governor's Palace in the center of town. It was such a splendid place and in grandeur, not unlike the royal palaces in London, though quite different in structure.

When we were greeted at the door, we gave our names and told the doorman that Governor Lee was expecting us.

I was almost shocked at how quickly and well we were received. Obviously the governor was serious about his offer!

**Gardens and Governor's Palace
Colonial Williamsburg**

Mr. Lee treated us as peers, sitting us in the grand parlor of that fabulous mansion. He had his personal servant bring us tea and made sure that we were comfortable. He unveiled to us how he had been granted by the Crown and the House of Burgesses the leadership of the colony in the absence of the Governor, Sir William Gooch, who had returned to England and was ill. Also, that in this position he was given charge of vast portions of Augusta County which were needed to be owned and controlled by capable colonists for development as tobacco plantations. A good number of the folk who had settled there were Scotch-Irish, immigrating to Virginia from Pennsylvania, Lee told us.

After we related our complete story, he had a parchment created of the grant from the King for 344 acres. It began on Crab Creek and Mile Branch of New River. In the late 1600s, we were told by Lee, a Dutch priest, Friar Hans, first arrived in the upper region. His name was taken for the community being formed there in the early 1700s.

He also told us that all free males living in Virginia between the ages of 16 and 50 were required to sign up for the Virginia Militia, which could be called upon at any time to defend the Crown. George was thrilled to do so, and the Governor had the papers prepared.

We thanked him from the bottom of our hearts and left that day feeling on top of the world. 344 acres! We couldn't believe it! Though we were but freeholders, we owned a large tract of land and in England we would now be considered the gentry, not just common poor folks like before.

Chapter Four

We returned to the inn and the next morning George and I went to the nearby stable and bought a team of large, sturdy Narragansett Pacer horses, from Rhode Island and a Conestoga wagon, which had been brought in from Lancaster County, Pennsylvania by migrants, with money I had brought. I let George have enough coins to pay for them because I could tell even then that he was resistant to my having money when he didn't, but at least he didn't demand to keep it all in his possession. I had earned it and though it now belonged to us as a married couple, I knew that I must maintain some control because of his lack of education and experience in finances.

The horses were the finest money could buy, and a Conestoga wagon was a new but effective way to travel and haul goods. Both were a bit extravagant, taking over half of my money. But I expected that this combination would be perfect for our journey. Some people were using oxen to pull their wagons, but for us, the horses would serve more than one purpose in our future.

Conestoga wagon or prairie schooner

As we drove out of the stable, George was staring at the brickyard across the street. All of Williamsburg had been built with bricks from that yard.

"Ya know, me love, I am goin' ta have ta build us a house. I'm a mason an' I'll have ta have bricks and I'll have ta make 'em meself."

And with that he drove directly across the street and parked as close as possible to the brickyard.

Going inside, he eyed the bottle type kiln very carefully. Then he asked one of the workers what he would need to build a small kiln of that style. He was told that it would require at least six hundred firebricks and a metal grate on which to burn the coal or wood. The price was actually more than we could afford. But I knew that George was right. And I knew that he only had built homes with bricks in England. He took me by the hand and asked me to go out a ways with him. He looked at me with his big grey eyes and I couldn't say no. It's a good thing we had bought that large wagon. It could stand the weight and hold the bricks with room left for us and the supplies we would buy along the way. We just must be careful on bumpy terrain. The workers loaded our materials and we were on our way.

George flipped the reigns and clicked his tongue, and the horses immediately responded.

"Hasn't the Crown been gracious to us, me love? Long live the King!" George was beaming as those words flowed from his lips. It seemed that he was trying to shift his thoughts away from his feelings of lack of monetary control.

"It is God's will," I said. "I am thankful."

That day we set off in our very own wagon for the great western territory of Augusta County and our new home! Luckily, the weather was ideal, and the cloth cover shaded us from the pouring streams of sunshine now almost directly over us as our large young horses sprinted across the verdant landscape on the stage coach road. It took till nightfall to reach the first major turn in the road going toward Richmond. Since we had our basic belongings in the wagon, and the cover to shelter us, we set up camp.

There was still just a hint of coolness in the night air, so we built a campfire near our wagon with the flint that we had stuck in our chest. Leaves and small sticks fueled the flames until we were able to burn larger pieces of dead limbs that we had found under the trees. Everything just felt right.

We had purchased some dried beans, a pone of bread and a hunk of salty ham in Williamsburg which made the first meal I had cooked in the New World. We would have enough left to do us until we reached Richmond. We both had canteens of water. What a fine life!

I felt my baby jump in my womb! Could this be happening already? Yet it was! I smiled and told George what I had experienced. He laid his head softly on my shoulder and sighed. All of our children would be born in this new and exciting frontier!

That night we snuggled close on the covers we had in the wagon and looked out on the moonlit beauty of this lovely land. A partially seeded tobacco field lay to our north and I could almost feel George's passionate desire. In a few years this would be the scene at our own farm.

The next morning early we packed up and drove into a plantation to obtain supplies for the next leg of our trip. The family was very caring and fed us some eggs, bacon, biscuits and coffee for breakfast; then, on we journeyed, across toward the Great Divide.

Later that morning a shower came in from the west and reminded us that it was indeed still April. The breeze blew a bit of it in on our faces, because we were driving directly into it; but it was pleasingly refreshing and we really didn't mind. We had no idea how far we had gone that first day; but the second day, according to the sign posts, we traveled eighteen miles. I thought we had made good time, especially with the rain we had gone through.

George was obviously happy about our good fortune, especially the land that we had been granted. But I still knew that he had no idea what would be coming before his dreams could become a reality, and neither did I!

We talked along our way about what we would do when we first arrived at our new home and how excited we both were about our future.

We were so looking forward to getting to our property that most of the obstacles we encountered seemed small. Even when we had to travel farther and wait longer to reach new fresh water supplies and buy more food. But that sense of anticipation began to wane as we got closer to our goal.

Chapter Five

It took us twenty-six days to arrive at our property. May was well spent. Besides the grant, we had been given the deed, of course, a plat and a map, of a sort. Directions, as good as could be given, were written down by a guide in the service of the governor before we left. He insisted that he lead us there, but we knew we couldn't afford his fee.

We were also told that our tract was adjoining John Craig's farm which ran south from the headwaters of Crab Creek. Craig had recently obtained a large tract of land to the north of us. The man who owned another adjoining tract to our east was named John Montgomery. We were to contact him, as he had already built a house there.

We had heard rumors, along the way, of strife with the Indians, in spite of supposed agreements which had been made. Indians, we had been told, frequently traveled through the valley but we were not informed of any major conflicts, as both the settlers and the Natives desired peace.

As we neared our property we had great difficulty following the trails and paths, probably made by Indians. There was no clearly defined road for several miles and no easy way into the community. Sometimes we had to choose between two trails to keep going. Now we realized why the guide was so insistent that he bring us. At one place we had to stop at a small cabin and ask for the proper way, thinking we must have missed something. Luckily, the man of the house had traveled along the western trail on horseback and was familiar with our destination. He had been to Hans Meadows once. George had to use his axe to cut small trees and brush from the trail to make it wide enough to continue with the wagon. Fording streams was difficult as well. I realized that buying the bricks had been a providential move in yet another way. It weighted down the wagon so that it would not capsize crossing rocky streams. Everyone we talked with along the way told us that they didn't believe that anyone had ever attempted to bring a wagon across this wilderness. Everyone had used packhorses to come in and out from the east.

When we finally arrived, we soon located John Montgomery, who told us his story. He was an immigrant from Donegal, Ulster, Ireland, who had come to Virginia from Lancaster, Pennsylvania in '46 when his father, James Montgomery, Senior, had sent him with his half brother Robert there to purchase land. They had originally bought 654 acres on Catawba Creek, several miles to our north. They had gone back to Lancaster and brought the entire family to that property and John and another half brother, William, had moved down here to Hans Meadows.

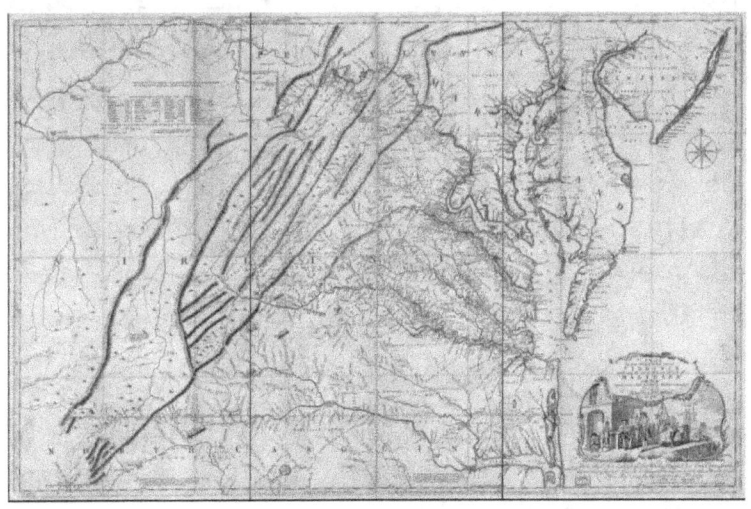

Fry- Jefferson Map, 1752

John just shook his head when we told him how we came across that wilderness with our wagon. He said that we were definitely the first ones to even attempt such a feat. But we were both determined. He told us that we should have gone to the north into Pennsylvania and taken the Great Wagon Road on down to Hans Meadows. But no one had told us about that. We had bought the Conestoga wagon for the journey and neither hell nor high water could have stopped us!

Now I understood why this area was being settled by Pennsylvania migrants.

Donegal, I later learned from John, means "fort of foreigners." It is a county in the very northeastern point of Ireland, and was inhabited largely by the O'Donnells, Ulster's second most powerful ruling clan, until the start of the 17th century. John told me that he was descended on his mother's line from them and had been taken as a boy to see the famed Donegal Castle.

John was just a few years older than we were, and yet unmarried, but told us that he was keeping company with a young girl, Ann Agnes Crockett, of whom he was quite fond and hoped to wed when she was of age. She went by Agnes, he told us.

Our property was largely wooded with the lovely Mile Creek surging beside it. Mr. Montgomery showed us on our plat that the creek defined our eastern border with his farm and told us that we needed to get a surveyor to completely lay our property out. From the description on the deed, the area was fairly well defined, so until we were able to pay a surveyor we would merely stay within the parameters which were clearest. Nobody had fenced their land here anyway.

Thankfully, we had purchased enough food supplies at our last stop to feed us for a few days, and as I said, an axe. George cleared out the rocks and leveled the ground along both sides to make fording it easier. There was also a spring at the top of a rolling hill on the eastern side of our place, where we could get our water, and a stream flowing from it into Mile Creek. George cleaned out the mud in the spring and lined it with small stones from the creek soon after we arrived. We had a metal pail and dipper we had bought when shopping for vegetables and meat on the way over.

There was a grassy area near the creek and the road coming in from the north large enough for a house and to graze our horses. It was just across the creek from the Montgomery house.

George spent most of the first day unloading the bricks and beginning work on building the kiln. That took him a full week. I was amazed at how it looked like just a smaller version of the one in Williamsburg. He was an excellent mason!

The day after the kiln was complete he began the gigantic task making bricks from mud in the creek and straw that John Montgomery provided for us from his last year's wheat crop. He was very talented in that way.

Reconstruction of large Colonial brick kiln

After he had baked a number of bricks in his kiln, George cut straight poplars and split logs for lumber. It was a painstaking and lengthy process. I was unable to help him, of course, but John and his half brother, William, who lived about a mile away, on the other end of their property, came and lent him a hand when they had some free time. Their father was living in the Catawba area, where Robert had also settled.

Of course it was still planting time for some vegetables and the Montgomerys were busy putting out their huge garden, so their availability for work with George was only occasional.

Even before the house was finished, George dug a deep hole about fifty yards behind the house and used some of the boards he had split to make a privy. We were all tired of going to the woods to relieve ourselves.

We still didn't know if George's uncle was locating near us, but it wasn't long till we found out.

Chapter Six

It took George over three months to get the house built and to construct some basic furniture, such as a feather bed, a rough board table and chairs made of small tree branches. John gave him enough nails to last until he could get more. I was pleased with all of his work. The bed was certainly more comfortable than the floor of the wagon or the house. And it was grand to have a real table to set our food on and something to sit down on while we enjoyed our meals.

George had to get out and meet the other settlers to scavenge the items we needed. We were able to get feathers from several farmers who had ducks and chickens. It was really great that George was a mason, not just because he was able to build a brick house for us, but also because he was able to construct a splendid fireplace with which we could warm and cook. He sealed it all extremely well.

Just about the time we got ourselves to staying in the house, George's uncle, Sam McGregor—that was his name—showed up at our door!

Where was he when we needed him? But he did bring us a peace offering! Two fine oak rockers and a baby bed made by the Amish in Lancaster! Needless to say, I forgave him immediately.

By asking around, he had found out where our house was. It turned out that he was only about ten miles away to our south. He had brought his son, Sammy, to help him build. He had gotten a frame home constructed, he told us, and they had been living in it for about a month.

We were also taken aback when we found out that Uncle Sam had met John Montgomery's father, James, in Lancaster. We marveled at what a small world it was after all!

Sam's visit was pleasurable, and he invited us to his home as soon as we were able to come. I was only a few months away from delivering my child, so I certainly wasn't going to travel on a bumpy road even that far. I had been through enough simply getting to our farm. He asked me when my "wee bairn was a comin'." He seemed excited for us.

I had contacted a young midwife named Cindy who lived in Hans Meadows who had examined me and promised to deliver the wee one. She told me that I was doing well and that the baby was a normal size for how far along I was.

I didn't understand why I was having strange cravings; but Cindy said that it was normal for women in my condition.

George had built a small rail horse lot for our Philly, Sugar and our stallion, Jake, while cutting trees for the boards needed for framing and flooring in our house.

There were plenty of wild grasses to last for a while, and the fence could be moved, if needed. He had also constructed a lean-to shelter to protect them from the brunt of a possible storm.

One day while I was out petting our horses I noticed a vine running over the ground which was edging its way up one of the fence posts. I leaned over to take a closer look, for I thought it may be poison ivy. Right away I realized that it wasn't, because it had five leaves on each stem, and poison ivy has but three.

The next time John came over I asked him what on earth it was, for we had seen nothing like it in England.

"I hadn't either," he said. "I call it Virginia Creeper! It is native to these parts and it seems to be creeping up about everything around my place!"

I smiled. "Sounds good to me!" I said.

We have sure seen a lot of "Virginia Creeper" since. We just cut it down. It's simply a small annoyance we have to deal with!

But another thing we have here that we never saw before is what they call pawpaw trees. There are some growing wild on our place. They have greenish little fruit that is great to eat. They taste a bit like custard, I think.

There are also plenty of blackberries, huckleberries and elderberries. Those I use to make jam and jelly.

The next two months were needed to get settled in and make sure that there were enough supplies to survive till we were able to buy more. George found odd jobs to do for other colonists to earn enough to pay for these. But actually being able to be a planter still seemed only a far-away dream—kinda like Papa's prophesy was when I was a girl. Clearing was a massive undertaking.

On 28 May, John told us that in early June, the entire Montgomery family property at Catawba had been deeded over to Robert by their father as he was the one living with him and helping on his farm.

Wouldn't you know it! It was during the rainy late night hours of Sunday, 3 October 1751 when I felt the pangs of childbirth bearing down on me and I woke George up to ride the two miles to get the midwife, Cindy.

Thank heavens, by the time they were back, my pains were awfully close together, and the preparations were barely complete when I gave birth to a fine blond-headed boy! I knew that he took his hair colour from my dear mama who was a lovely Dutch lady. We had already agreed that if I had a male he would be called Michael for George's father. We knew we would likely never see him again—I had never laid eyes upon him—but we could write to him and let him know. Well, I did, since George couldn't read or write. But it was a long time before we were finally able to get our letters out. I will explain later.

I thought there had never been so handsome a child. I pressed him to my face, and then to my bosom, where he drank in his first nourishment in the open world. The New World of Virginia!

Chapter Seven

Winter was upon us, and our care for Michael took preeminence over clearing new ground. That winter we had several deep snows. The worst one covered our shake-shingled roof with a heavy blanket and drifted half way up our front door! But we were very happy.

Progress was slow, of course. In the next two years George was able to get the rest of the first ten acres cleared with the help of Sammy, lent to him on occasion by Uncle Sam, and John Montgomery's brother, William. The stumps were the worst to get out. Then, of course, there was burning the trees we didn't use for firewood and boards. They would work each year until the weather got so cold they couldn't stand staying out for very long.

This method was employed until George learned the "firebrand" system. He then used his axe to cut around the outer layer of the trees and kill them. Then after the trees were dead they were set on fire and burned up right there in the ground.

It felt so wonderful to see everything falling into place! I did all I could to make our house a real home. And we were making preparations for the enlargement of our family.

Settlers clearing land

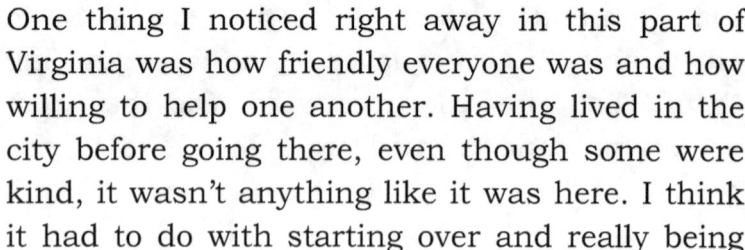

One thing I noticed right away in this part of Virginia was how friendly everyone was and how willing to help one another. Having lived in the city before going there, even though some were kind, it wasn't anything like it was here. I think it had to do with starting over and really being able to have something of their own. Part of it may have been due to the fact that most of them were from Northern Ireland. I knew that I would feel at home here for the rest of my days.

But with all the time that George had been spending with other men around the area, his attitude toward women—and even toward me—began to change, and not for the better. Women in the colonies initially had no rights. They were to stay home and keep out of men's affairs. Though things had improved somewhat in the 18th century in the places of culture, rural areas were behind the times.

This bothered me. I was not a simple mountain girl who had been brought up in the country. Though to some extent women were still viewed as inferior in England, those who worked and supported themselves were revered. George's changes in attitude were depressing; but being strong, I soldiered on.

Nevertheless, almost every year was to bring a new child into our family. That particular year, 1752, on December 20th, our darling James came along. He was so different from Michael! A head full of dark hair like his father! Mine was a chestnut brown. Still, he was a precious baby, of course. It was more responsibility, but so worth it. It was just that now my work was increasing and I realized that I might as well get used to it. I let my boys keep my mind on a positive note.

Time was passing so quickly now. On 28 November of '53, John invited us to his and Agnes' wedding. I had several lengths of cloth that I had brought from a traveling merchant from Pennsylvania with which I made our undress clothing, and I had gotten a strip of nice violet linen material to make myself a dress to wear on special occasions. I'm so glad that I had! I made everything myself, even my petticoat and a dress bonnet. Agnes was just amazed at how nice that dress looked on me! At least that's what she told me. And I thought I did a pretty darn good job on it myself.

They were married by a Presbyterian minister in Agnes' parents' spacious home about four miles away from us. They had a wonderful party afterward! I had never attended such an extravagant gala! The Crocketts were well-healed and fit into the local society with the Craigs, but the Montgomerys were also very highly thought of around here. I wasn't used to drinking champagne, but I did sample a tad at that wedding. I noticed that there was also a vial of Scotch whisky being consumed by John Craig and his close friends. Craig was now building a huge log house on his sprawling farm.

I did appreciate the Montgomerys taking us in like a part of their own clan. We were forming a bond that would only grow stronger with time.

It was the third year before George was able to begin planting a field of corn. He got a plow and hoe from Uncle Sam. The soil had to be grubbed up into fine dirt with a hoe before rows could be plowed in which to plant the seed corn. This was a long, exhausting process.

Corn was the most practical first crop, as Sugar and Jake could eat corn, as well as our Guernsey cow, Bossie, that George had bought from John. We would also be acquiring hogs and chickens, all which could consume a lot of corn. Corn was also needed for meal for bread.

The land was so rich and fertile here that we were in awe at how well our corn grew and how much it produced. George spread cow manure lightly in the rows to fertilize the corn even better.

The agreement we had signed had allowed us up to ten years before we were required to begin planting tobacco, as long as improvements were made to the land and crops were being planted.

On 28 May 1754, a twenty-two year old officer, whom no one around us seemed to know, named George Washington, had been sent by the Governor of Virginia at the time, Robert Dinwiddie, as an envoy to the French, warning them to stay away from the area of Pennsylvania directly to our north, in the Alleghenies. The French refused, and on his way home, on 3 July, Washington's men became embroiled in a skirmish with a French encampment known as the Battle of Jumonville Glen, in which the French ensign, Joseph Coulon de Jumonville was killed.

Washington ordered his men to construct a fort for their protection there, naming it, quite appropriately, Fort Necessity. The ensuing incident, the Battle of the Great Meadows, coupled with the previous one, sparked what became known as the French and Indian War. It ended up as an international conflict called the Seven Years' War. Great Meadows at Fort Necessity was Washington's first career defeat.

This war greatly affected all of us in the Allegheny Mountains. It involved various Indian tribes fighting with both sides, but we were fortunate that those who lived in our section of the state all fought with the British. The Northern Indian tribes who fought with the French, however, devastated the more exposed sections of our county. But I would find out later that incidents with the Shawnees occurred all too close to us.

The most awful thing we heard about happened not too far to our north, at Draper Meadows. Shawnees invaded the small settlement, killing a number of the residents and capturing the rest, taking them far west into the part of the state known as Kentucky. No one knew how far they had gone, but hunters saw signs of their journey along the river. This made me apprehensive. I couldn't even imagine what those folks were going through.

Sometime around the late fall of '55 news reached us that one of the young women captured at Draper Meadows had escaped and managed to get home. She was one of the family for which the community was named. Her name was Mary Draper Ingles.

Going back a few months, I was overly excited for Agnes Montgomery when she gave birth to her first child, Esther, on 5 February in '55. I had introduced her to Cindy, who was happy to have another customer.

Esther was a darling little red-head, and I know John loved her a lot, because I saw his eyes brighten every time he came into the room where she was. Agnes and I now had more in common and she asked me questions about what I did about this and that with my children.

John Montgomery was always respectful of me. He served as a Captain during the French and Indian War and commanded a company of Volunteers, incorporated with part of the Virginia Regiment on the Shawnee expedition in 1756, under command of Major Andrew Lewis. Lewis was serving under Colonel George Washington.

General Andrew H. Lewis

Another of John's half brothers, Joseph, served in his company of Volunteers, on that same expedition.

Their father, James, had also served as a Justice in the Augusta County Court, a Militia Captain and an officer of the New Derry Presbyterian congregation. He was one of the most prominent men in the community. But he died in November '56 before he could be properly rewarded for all he had done. His wife soon returned to Pennsylvania, taking some of her children with her.

Though he was chomping at the bits to go, George was not called upon to serve in this conflict. And I was glad.

French and Indian War

Chapter Eight

I was beginning to think that our union could only produce male offspring when in October '56, on the 10th of that month, our daughter Barbara was brought into the world. I was so thrilled that I could have jumped for joy, were it possible! George was less enthused. Like most men, I suppose, to begin with he was thinking about boys to keep the family name going and help on the farm.

But girls have a way of piercing the heart of a man, and Barbara was no exception. Blonde hair and soft blue eyes like my mother. The older boys made over her as much as younguns can.

That year news reached us of a new breed of horses being introduced into the Virginia colony. A planter named Mordecai Booth had some time back imported from England a ten-year-old Chestnut Thoroughbred named Janus. He was a smaller horse, standing just about 14 hands, but well muscled. The article I read said that he had especially powerful hindquarters. He had also been a race horse in England, and had become a successful racer in the James River area. But an injury had retired him to stud.

I have continued to follow his story because I love horses so much. After this, mares which he sired became distinguished racing mares. After being bred to quarter racing stock, his brilliance truly was recognized. Janus became known as the "Father of the Quarter Horse."

Michael was already forming his personality and I was so pleased. He was a "Mama's boy," probably because I made him feel special. He was very smart, and talented in everything, it seemed. At only three years old he had learned how to read and write, learned his alphabet and several rhymes that I learned in London when I first started school. At six he was helping me teach James. He also loved drawing with a piece of charcoal on a slate that I had brought with me from the old country. I taught the children to write with a quill pen and juice from poke-berries. I knew that he was a special little angel sent from God to help me. In fact, Michael means "gift from God" in Hebrew.

Getting back, on 12 February '57, Agnes' and John's second child came along. This was the first of their boys, and they named him James after his Grandpa Montgomery. They would eventually have a very large family—fourteen in all!

I was visiting with Agnes one day in their home when I noticed a small booklet lying on their kitchen table. I picked it up and saw that it was called *"Poor Richard, an Almanack for the Year 1749."* I couldn't resist flipping through it. It had weather forecasts and puzzles and was filled with witty and humorous sayings. On the front it said that it was published by Richard Saunders in Philadelphia and sold by B. Franklin.

"What do you know about the fellow who wrote this book?" I asked Agnes.

She laughed. "Poor Richard is what Benjamin Franklin calls himself. He's a publisher and socialite in Pennsylvania. We got accustomed to reading his almanacks when we were in Lancaster. Too bad we can't get it down here."

I think I like this fellow, I thought to myself.

We didn't have any more live births in our family for the next couple of years, but I lost one which was stillborn and another which I miscarried. The sadness and pain are still very real, and really never go away. I hurt so badly. Of course I had my boys to share the loss with me. I knew George felt it too, but it seemed somehow he was becoming callused. I guess things like that can change a man.

George stayed busy with the crops and the animals and our flock of chickens was growing quickly. Our neighbors shared eggs with us to set from various breeds and we had a healthy flock by then.

Michael and James loved helping around the house and tending to the chickens. This is a bit off-subject, but neither of them would ever be very tall. Well, with both of their parents being about the same height—about five-foot two— what chance did we have of producing tall sons?

Our roosters would make sure we didn't sleep too late in the mornings because the chickens had free reign of the place and roosted in trees near the house. We had hickory trees, maples and a large chestnut tree near the house. I told the boys to be careful where they stepped, as they were barefooted most of the time.

Little by little we were able to get all the things we needed for our farm. We bought English saddles for both horses, as they were the only type we could find. They must have been the only type in Virginia.

The boys loved to ride our horses, so we would saddle them up, lift the boys up onto them and lead them around the fields.

The winters weren't too frigid around that time. The deepest snow in the winter of '58 was only about 10 inches and that came in early March.

I took notes on the weather just like I had done with the first steps and words of my younguns. Michael was talking by the time he was 16 months old. I couldn't understand why they all said "Papa" before "Mama!" I was with them a lot more than George was!

I loved our family being together more in the winters because during the busy times when crops were being made and harvested we were all running around like chickens with their heads cut off. And that's how we killed our roosters for the pot, by the way. George kept his axe sharp by rubbing it on a large sandstone from the creek. We didn't kill the hens because we needed them to lay eggs and hatch biddies.

Those years seemed to fly by—and then it was '59. Oh, what dreadful a year!

Chapter Nine

The flowers were beginning to bloom once again in the Virginia colony and we had planted a lot of bulbs because the blooms came back every spring and they multiplied. I was able to get them from Agnes, who had, in turn, been given her start by other ladies in the community. I wished that she had had some tulip bulbs, but no such luck. These ladies had never been so blessed as to live in my colourful homeland of Holland.

Agnes had given birth to her second son, John Junior, near the end of January in that fateful year of Our Lord, 1759.

Then on May 8th, another welcome package arrived in our home, as Cindy aided in the delivery of our second beautiful lass, Elizabeth Ann. The Ann part was in honor of my dear friend, Agnes.

We didn't know where her bright red hair came from, but we figured it could have been the Scottish blood of the McGregors coming out. At any rate, she was very comely but would go through the awkward stage with having too many freckles. Cindy said she had been christened by a baker. That was a common saying back then. She had gorgeous green eyes like a cat I had had when I was a young girl in Holland. I don't know why I thought of that sweet cuddly kitty unless it was because it not only had green eyes, but was a golden tabby on the edge of red.

We loved our little family and we now had children ranging in age from a tiny infant to eight years of age. Michael already wanted to go with his father to the fields and to the little barn that George had built, to help milk Bossie. Luckily we were able to get her bred each year, and we kept the calves to fatten.

Maybe it was time for a puppy dog. At least Michael said it was. James, quite naturally, agreed.

But that year the most horrible thing I could imagine happened! No, I shan't say that. I could never have imagined such a horror! It came to be known as the epidemic of 1759. It started in Winchester and fear and panic spread even to other towns and communities. George had met with a man who had come all the way down from Winchester about farm business, who must have unknowingly been in the early stages and brought the dread disease here with him. I really never knew why that fellow would come so far, but George said he was talking to farmers all over the state about new ways of farming and tools being produced to make the work easier.

George started feeling hot, getting sweaty and breaking out, so he stayed in the house. Though he was only mildly affected, our baby girls were most vulnerable. Both of them came down with a horrible case of pox. They had excessive body heat and that awful skin rash that kept spreading.

Some doctors in Winchester, we were told, were experimenting with what they called "inoculations," but a lot of people were leery of them. There was no doctor around Hans Meadows and certainly no real cure. Both girls died that November. I cried till I felt there could be no moisture left in my body. I did have to go to the spring more often, and drank a powerful lot of water.

George blamed himself, but that is one thing he could have had no knowledge about and was certainly not guilty of.

We buried our two beautiful little lassies on a grassy knoll about a stone's throw from our house and this was the start of our Walters family cemetery. Their graves are marked by fieldstones.

Doctor examining a baby during the epidemic of 1759

Chapter Ten

One day in July the boys were playing I Spy in the yard. One of them would hide and the other would try to find him. All of a sudden, John Montgomery came strolling along carrying a darling black and white Shepherd pup in his hands. Someone had likely gone begging! What could I say? I called out for George and when he walked sheepishly up he was grinning from ear to ear. Now I knew that he was involved in this veiled conspiracy! We named the dog Shep and our younguns loved him. He was a great pet and companion for the boys and followed Michael everywhere he went.

We were getting quite a blend of creatures on our farm. Sugar and Jake had been a true blessing; George needed a team, not only for pulling the wagon, but also for plowing. Bossie was providing milk for us; her calves would supply veal. The chickens were keeping us in eggs and we even had a few guineas now. We had also just bought a shoat for fattening.

That year, George was able to sow two acres in wheat. Our first little crop of it! He also grew a little over two acres of Timothy for hay.

George had learned how to split off the outsides of logs to make outbuildings. As I mentioned, he had built a fine little barn. He had also erected a pig sty and a cozy chicken house with several nests filled with dried leaves.

We would also be butchering a hog every winter for pork, so he was now putting up a smokehouse in which to hang, salt and smoke the meat.

While he was labouring away on the smokehouse, Michael took Shep out into the woods. Shep caught the scent of a frisky squirrel and kept running farther and farther away from our house to the south, along Mile Creek. Somehow the squirrel, in his effort to escape Shep, turned to the west and before long Michael had no idea where he was or how to get back home. It was late in the day, and darkness had begun to fall. By this time George was milking Bossie. I went out to the barn and asked him if he had seen Michael lately. Of course, he hadn't.

I was getting frantic. George had been so engrossed in building that he had no thought on which direction those two had headed, he said.

"Michael! Michael!" I cried.

"Hya Shep! Hya Shep!" George yelled.

Yet all we heard was the distant rushing of Mile Creek and a whippoorwill crying from far to the north.

George then suddenly remembered seeing Shep following Michael down the creek bank, and he headed out in a run.

As the moon rose slowly over the mountain to our east, I simply asked God to please bring our son home. My heart beat rapidly and I felt faint.

James came out of the house crying. He knew what was going on; how could he not? The minutes felt like hours. I started pacing the porch of our cabin. I knew I must stay there with James. I sure couldn't take him with me into those dark woods. No sir! I wasn't about to.

James ran into my arms and I hugged him close. It took a few minutes to get him somewhat calmed down and his tears dried.

It was almost an hour later when a bedraggled George and Michael emerged into the dim light of our cabin. I wanted to cut a hickory switch and whip his behind soundly! But in this case, I knew I mustn't. I was sure that George had already spanked him with his hard hand. That was enough.

"Michael," I said sternly, "don't you ever scare us like that again! I let you keep Shep for a pet. He isn't really a hunting dog. Don't ever go very far from home again!"

"But Mama! I couldn't let Shep get away! And he did tree a squirrel!"

"Shep is a dog! He knows his way home, son," I scolded.

Michael stopped, turned his eyes upward toward mine and told me he was sorry, and that he would never do it again.

It took us all quite a while to get to sleep that night, but thank the good Lord; we never had that incident repeated.

Pioneer Smokehouse

Chapter Eleven

In late December 1760 I received a long, dreadful letter from my brother, Christopher. He had found out where we were through the House of Burgesses. The letter had been sent through the British Imperial Post, and I was terribly surprised that I had gotten it. I likely wouldn't have if it hadn't been marked "urgent." It had taken two months to arrive, and had been delivered by a military currier.

First, he told me that Papa had quit work to care for our frail mama a few months earlier. She had declined quickly and passed away about a month before his letter was written.

My poor papa had been so distraught that he had turned to drinking. That proud, religious man who had seen visions and predicted my future had turned to the bottle? I just couldn't believe it! Why had neither my brother nor my sister tried to let me know sooner?

He said that Papa had had no money to give Mama a decent burial, so she had been laid to rest in a shroud directly in the ground in Cross Bones Cemetery for paupers in South London!

Oh, my God! How could I stand this? Wasn't losing my girls enough?

Then he said that Papa was found stiff and dead on a city bench covered only with a dirty old sheet. Now they were burying him beside my poor mama!

I just threw myself over the bed and wept so hard that I thought I would surely die! Now Papa would never know about the grandsons he had, the girls we lost, or any of our other children!

Finally I was able to return to read the rest of that horrid letter.

Next, he told me of the death of King George II of the Royal House of Hanover at age 76, and the fact that his grandson, the Duke of York, was succeeding him on the throne.

My hysterical husband cried more about the passing of the King than the death of my precious parents! He came in a little of not going out to work the next day. He could be both strong and tender when it came to those he cared a lot for. Well, then there is stubborn.

The King's wife, Caroline of Anspach, Christopher wrote, had predeceased him, and he was buried by her side at Westminster.

His successor had become George III. The name and the House of Hanover would continue. This much pleased my George after I could stop crying long enough to tell him.

But we had no inkling of what was to come during his reign. Still, George stayed loyal to the Crown.

Christopher, obviously, was badly broken. He was so saddened about what happened to our parents and disgusted with their meager existence in London that he didn't want to remain there any longer.

He told me that Sophia, though very stricken, wanted to stay in London. She had met a nice young man who would be a comfort to her, and who may end up as her life mate.

I was able to send word to Christopher in a letter that I had given to John who had a family connection, a cousin on his mother's side who had moved here from Lancaster with close connections in the government, who could get it to Williamsburg, where it would be sent on to

London. I had told him of the good lands here and our progress in the Virginia colony.

I let him know about the arrangement I now had with John to get mail sent between us. He wrote back asking if I knew anyone who could sponsor him. We were not yet able to pay his and his family's passage over, so I went to John and Agnes and asked if they could do it in return for work for them. They looked at one another and John asked if I could give them a few days to talk it over.

The very next morning John came over and told me that he would do it for a five year indenture. After all, there were four of them and though the children would be less of a cost, the extra funds must be considered.

John sent a letter by his cousin who took it on his next trip to the House of Burgesses. It was then given to a ship captain who was taking tobacco to London. Through slow communications John made arrangements to pay him when he safely delivered them to Norfolk.

As soon as I could think carefully about what I should say to him, I wrote to Christopher and had John send it by his cousin like before. In April they arrived in the port at Norfolk.

We had recently bought a buggy for short trips, but it was only good for three people. Of necessity, John and George traveled there in our Conestoga wagon to greet them and bring them here. By that time we had a passable road going to the coastal area. The widened Indian trails that George had cut had been used and improved by others.

Somewhat in control of my emotions by then (at least able to face them without tears), I was thrilled when they finally arrived! They stayed with us and slept temporarily in the barn loft in the soft hay with covers which I gave them. George had harvested the Timothy which he had grown the year before with a scythe. There was also straw on the other side of the loft which was left after the grains were removed from wheat.

George was happy to add a room onto our house in which they slept after he finished building it in late May. Christopher and Emma were very grateful. Christopher was already working with John by that time, doing odd jobs around his farm.

But another sad thing happened right after they moved in here. Our beloved cow, Bossie died and we all worked together to dig a grave deep enough to bury her in the meadow. We have truly missed her.

Right away George bought a young Jersey heifer which he named Ginger. The farmer who sold her to George had a fine bull, and she could have calves and supply milk.

We had made arrangements directly with the House of Burgesses to accept all posts for us that were sent by John's cousin. I guess we were the most fortunate families in Hans Meadows to have such an arrangement. In early July Christopher and I received an up-beat letter from Sophia saying that she had indeed married her suitor, a bloke named Les Baxter, who was taking up the practice of law! The two, she said, were very devoted to one another, and she was so glad that she had waited until she was more mature to marry. She was almost twenty-seven. Now we would not be concerned as to her future.

George had been able to raise all of the corn, and now wheat, that we needed and we were able to sell some corn to other folks. A ways to our northwest, on Crab Creek, the Lattimers had built a grist mill in 1750, the very year in which we had arrived. That is where we had our corn and wheat ground. Now that was perfect timing! It was a far piece to get there but well worth it. It was the first mill in these parts.

George now had twenty-five acres in cultivation; a little more was being cleared each year when the crops were laid by. Once we had forty acres cleared we would be permitted to grow tobacco and fulfill our contract with the Virginia House of Burgesses.

Lattimer's Old Mill in 1906

Chapter Twelve

In the next few years our family grew by leaps and bounds! Four more boys came into our lives. William Curtis was our next son, born on 15 March 1766. He was a little butterball. His cheeks were as pink as carnations in fullest bloom; his hair, chestnut, like mine, and his skin a lovely tan colour. The other boys carried on over him like he was gold bullion.

I well recall how the others used to gather around his crib and reach in and tickle him and make him laugh and gurgle. Another thing that Michael loved to do was pinch his cute cheeks and make faces at him! My, how vivid those memories come back to me when I think of my Michael!

It seemed like but a few weeks, but over another year had flown by when George Anthony was born on 14 June in '67. I guess my husband finally broke me down about having a son named for him. Of course for me there was the burden of labour, but I didn't mind for the great reward. George had raven black hair and grey eyes like his papa, so I guess we picked the right one to be his namesake. George took to him so much from the very first time he saw him, especially when I told him that we were indeed christening him George II. I know it made him think of the King who had allowed us to have the land. My hubby would pick him up and put his lips to his little tummy and blow, making funny noises and the other boys would toss their heads back and roar with laughter.

Brown-haired John came on James' birthday; 20 December the next year then nature took a little break. You can't guess who I named him after! George got the idea that he was named for our neighbor, so he asked me and I confirmed it. I told him it meant nothing, and since I had named our daughter Elizabeth Ann for his wife, my best friend, it was only a courtesy.

Our last child, Jacob, was born on 3 July in '75. Jacob once again had light coloured hair and complexion. Actually, his hair was like sand on the beach. Seeing our boys, folks wouldn't even realize they were all members of the same family! I made sure that I didn't let Jacob get spoiled just because he was the baby of the family and we would never have another. I really didn't know that he would be the last. Of course they were all spoiled to some extent. But they all were treated as much alike as we knew how to do. Not that I hadn't always been partial to Michael. But George was biased toward Georgie.

Each child brought both new joy and new challenges. I had my hands full, for certain. Michael helped with William and George. He always wanted to be of assistance with everything I did. But my children were my pride and joy and my main reason for facing each new day. By the time Jacob came along, James and William were old enough to help me in the house.

Not long before the birth of our John, in early 1768, I read about a massive land survey that had been conducted over the past few years by two gentlemen named Charles Mason and Jeremiah Dixon to resolve a border dispute between Maryland, Delaware and Pennsylvania. In the article I read it said that the dispute had actually been caused by confusing differences in a proprietary grant by King Charles I to Lord Baltimore almost a hundred years earlier and a later grant from Charles II to William Penn. I don't know why I didn't learn about it until it was completed. I guess I just hadn't seen a newspaper back when it started. I suppose that was before they were easier to get around here.

But it has become an important part of our history now, and created what is known as the Mason-Dixon Line, separating the northern states from those in the South.

Mason and Dixon Surveying the Line

Getting back to family matters, Christopher had finished his indenture with John Montgomery in '66 and as a part of his contract he received fifty acres of land. Being deeded a piece of property was a common practice with indentures in those days. An added reward for completing the bargain. Like putting frosting on a cake.

I kept their children, Christy and Ethel, while Christopher and Emma worked together building a cabin of logs which George helped them cut. It was a genuine pleasure having them around. I felt even more at ease with blood kin living here.

They had brought two more children into the world since they arrived in Virginia: William and Anna. Yes, another William; but a Crewey, not a Walters. Thank God for Cindy!

I don't know how they managed while they were sleeping in our loft, but Emma had done a great job of making it comfortable, and dividing it into rooms with sheets hung from the rafters. They were staying in our house when the children were born, though.

It was good for our younguns having first cousins living here with whom to play and enjoy.

Chapter Thirteen

John Craig had completed his huge log house in early 1754. John had sold off a lot of his land and moved to Abingdon, Virginia in the 1770s after one of his sons was killed by Indians. I didn't know them well at the time, only by reputation. But what a shame that was! I don't even know how much land he had back then, but it was a pretty plenty. However, another of his sons, James, had been deeded the balance of John's property and obtained additional tracts of land on his own. He had developed a well-run farm which he had named Hans Meadow Plantation. James also opened and ran a prosperous tavern. His tavern became the central meeting place for the growing community and his influence had become remarkably strong.

In the summers George and I started taking outings with the children, though it was difficult getting them all settled in the wagon. They wanted to move around and argue with one another as to where they would each sit. Michael and James liked to fuss about which one would sit beside me and "ride shotgun," like on a stage coach. They had never even seen one at that time, but had heard John and Agnes talking about them and telling stories to their children.

In August of '77, after little George was born, we packed all the younguns up and went to Styles Falls, a very high waterfall on Purgatory Creek to our east. It was still difficult getting there over the newly built rough wagon road and it took us all morning. We couldn't all go to see the falls, because it was two miles off the road. George parked our wagon and we ate a picnic lunch of baked chicken, green beans and biscuits that I had cooked in our fireplace.

George took Michael and James and hiked all the way up there. They were bubbling over with excitement when they got back!

There were no schools anywhere around here, so I taught them all at home. I had brought a few books with me from London that I studied in at school and borrowed some from neighbors.

Every once in a while Uncle Sam and his family came to see us. You know, I never got around to visiting them at their home. George went once or twice. It seemed there were always too many younguns to care for and I was always cooking or washing out clothes in the creek. Life on a farm is a satisfying one, if you like it, but always a busy one.

Sam sat around with George when he wasn't in the field and they talked about things that happened back in the United Kingdom and all that was going on now with both of them and their families. I tried to keep his wife, Ella, entertained. She didn't talk much; it seemed like she never knew what to say to me. She was just in her own little world. And her accent was about like the Scottish folks I had met in London; worse than George's and even Sam's. I was always kinda glad when they left.

In the spring of 1761 our clearing requirement had been reached. George had pushed himself very hard to get it done. We had contacted the House of Burgesses by British Imperial Mail and ordered our seedlings to begin our plantation. In this case it was not necessary to use John's cousin. The mail had to go be delivered to Fort Chiswell by horseback and be taken by militia through Pennsylvania. It was guaranteed to be delivered because it was marked official business. The seedlings, of course, also arrived by way of the north passage through Pennsylvania.

That first year we were only able to put twenty acres in tobacco, but it was a great start. The rest was needed for meadow, grain crops and our large garden. There is still nothing like fresh vegetables out of your own garden. I used to love picking tomatoes and eating one right there with the juice running down my face!

We were on our way to true success, and I hoped, even greater happiness.

Farming in Colonial Virginia

Chapter Fourteen

Had it not been for our privileged arrangements of delivery of letters abroad we would have had no way to communicate with my family in England in those early years. As I have made quite clear, there was, of course, no organized postal service in the American Colonies. The British Imperial Post for most purposes was undependable and we couldn't just send letters out from or get them into Hans Meadows.

Because of the American Revolution it became imperative to have good post service. In 1765 the Stamp Act was passed and it sent an uproar through the colonies. One thing we did have was word of mouth about important happenings. I will get back to this a bit later.

An important couple which I first met right after they moved to the area in 1769 was Thomas and Clara Burke. They came around to our home to introduce themselves one day in early April to let everyone know that they had bought 200 acres from Jacob Shell on Crab Creek near the northwest end of the Craig place. I had met Jacob Shell when he came by to talk with

George about making him some bricks to underpin his porch. He had rock columns under the house and porch, and had built a rock fireplace, but he felt the bricks would look better and be nice as supports and to build a set of steps going up onto the porch.

The Burkes were young and had been married for eight years. They brought their three children with them in their buggy. Their names were Mary, John and Rebecca. We both wanted to do anything we could to help them get started here.

Thomas told us that his father, William Burke, had settled there in Augusta County in 1743, and had acquired 5600 acres. His papa had been killed by Indians when he was only thirteen years old.

"We children were put in the care of John Madison and his wife," he said.

"I am so sorry to hear that," I said. "What about your parents, Clara?" I asked.

"Well, that's another sad story." Clara sighed. "My papa was Doctor Robert Frazier. My mama was also named Clara. She was the daughter of Robert Graham, an English earl who disowned her when she fell in love with Papa, a poor doctor who had not yet built a practice. He wanted her to marry a rich member of the nobility. They followed their hearts, got married and came to America."

"Now that is a nice story," I said. "Where are your parents now? We could sure use a doctor around here!"

"They stayed in Pennsylvania."

Clara reminded me so much of my own dear mother when I was young. She had such lovely golden locks hanging down on her shoulders. Her head was covered on top with a pale blue bonnet that matched her beautiful linen dress. Her skin was also pale like my dear mama's, and she wore bright white gloves that made her look like the princess she almost was.

I asked them in for a cup of tea, and we got acquainted even better, sharing more adventures with one another. Such a lovely couple! And their children were exceptionally well mannered. She said she was going to make sure that Lord Robert, her grandfather, would be proud of their raising.

It was a while before we heard from them again, but there is so much more to their story.

Between 1770 and 1776 our county underwent three splits. Augusta County Virginia was a vast territory. It had originally extended westward from where we had settled on the Great Allegheny Divide, or Eastern Continental Divide, all the way to the Mississippi River. The waters which drain the area split here, with some streams flowing east, some west.

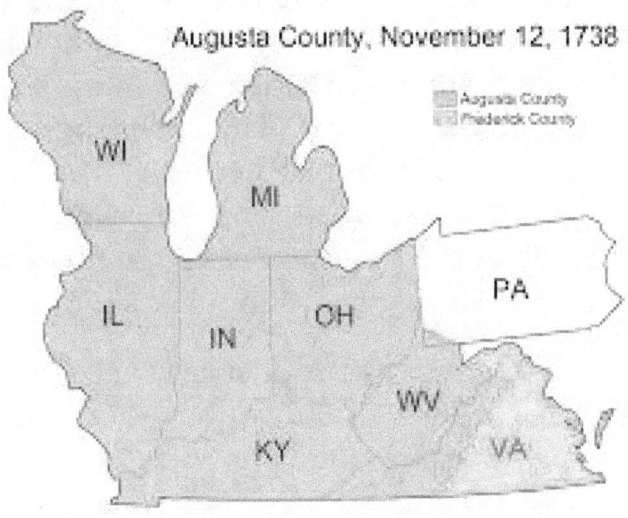

On 31 January 1770 the Act of Division created Botetourt County, named for Norborne Berkley, Lord Botetourt. It originally included all of Augusta County west of what would become the town of Lexington, Virginia.

From 15 February to 25 May of '71, John served as a justice of the peace for Botetourt County. He was following in his father's footsteps.

At that point John bought 664 acres near Buffalo Lick on Reed Creek from a man named Thomas Walker. He sold 125 acres of that to his half brother, William in '71.

Less than two years later, John served on a committee which split Fincastle County off of Botetourt, named for Governor John Murray, Earl of Dunmore's family estate, which included our community of Hans Meadows. The county seat was designated as Fort Chiswell on the north side of the New River, and the first county court was held there on 6 January 1773.

John was serving as the Justice of the Chancery Court in Botetourt County that year and was spending a lot of time in Fort Chiswell. He always filled me in on what was going on in the government when he was home, though. He could tell that I had a keen interest in politics.

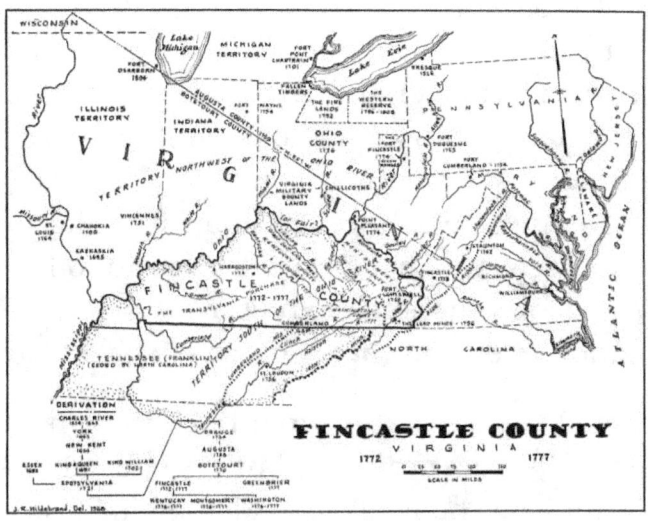

The British government had been deeply in debt as a result of the millions of pounds sterling that were spent winning the French and Indian War and its sister conflict, the Seven Years War, all of which ended in 1763. The Townshend Acts provoked oppression and unrest here in the colonies, which led to the Boston Massacre in 1770 and the Boston Tea Party in 1773.

As a result, in '74, the British government issued a proclamation which they named The Intolerable Acts, intended to punish the Massachusetts colonists for their defiance of the increased taxation of Britain on the colonies.

On 20 January 1775 a group of Fincastle County freeholders convened at Fort Chiswell, three months after the Battle of Point Pleasant when many of us had lost faith in Governor Dunmore. A Committee of Safety was set up with Justice William Christian as chairman, which drew up the Fincastle Resolutions. The freeholders therein expressed their determination to defend their rights with their lives.

I wanted George and me to attend, though it was quite a distance from us; but he refused, telling me that he had all confidence in Governor Dunmore and wanted nothing to do with this "ridic'les uprising."

Dunmore then made a treaty with the Shawnee Indians by which they gave up their hunting rights in the part of Virginia known as Kentucky and promised not to bother boats traveling on the Ohio River. Encouraged, a good number of settlers rushed into the area called Kentucky. By 1776, we were later told, there were 600 permanent settlers there.

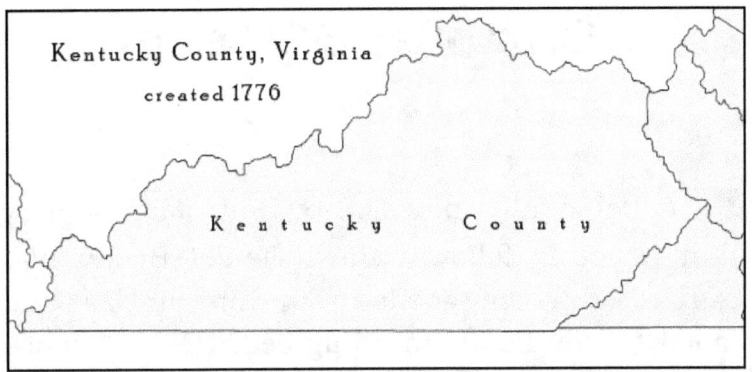

Kentucky County became the state of Kentucky on June 1, 1792

Chapter Fifteen

I was personally informed by John Montgomery that a young fellow named Daniel Boone had purchased some goods from him in '74 and failed to pay for them as agreed. He had sworn out a warrant for Boone under the authority of the King, but the scoundrel had slipped away and gone to Kentucky. I would never have believed he could have amounted to anything, but some people do change. Later Boone sent the money back to John.

I always kept a log of important events in the colonies. That year, 1774, from 5 September to 26 October, the First Continental Congress convened in Carpenter's Hall in Philadelphia, the seat of the Congress in Pennsylvania. All colonies except Georgia sent delegates which they had elected. The colonies were not all united; some sought a resolution with England, but some of them were very defensive of colonial rights.

Virginia's delegation was made up of a most even mix, but presented the most eminent group of men in America: Colonel George Washington,

Richard Henry Lee, Patrick Henry, Edmund Pendleton, Colonel Benjamin Harrison, Richard Bland, and the head of the lot was Peyton Randolph, who was elected President of the Continental Congress. He was to be the first in a long line of Presidents of Congress who would be the leaders our nation, even after the Revolution, before we began electing Presidents of these United States. These would include real patriots like Cyrus Vance and General Arthur St. Clair, a close friend of George Washington who was responsible for the formation of the state of Ohio.

This convention was determined that Parliament must be made to understand the grievances of the colonies and this body had to do everything possible to communicate them to all of America and the rest of the world.

On Wednesday, 14 June 1775 the Continental Congress placed the militia at Boston under its control, authorizing ten additional companies of riflemen to be raised. The following day they offered Colonel Washington a commission as "General and Commander in Chief of the Continental Army." This officially launched what became the United States Army.

On 16 October the Declaration and Resolves established the course of the Congress. It was a statement of principles common to all of the colonies. Though they were few in number and lacked the power to go up against the British Army, the stage had been set.

On the 20th of that month came The Association, patterned after our Virginia Association. It was set to become effective on 1 December. It would establish mechanisms throughout the colonies to enforce and regulate the resistance to Great Britain and keep the channels of communication open.

Philadelphia   Carpenters' Hall

Our local people were also determined to elect two delegates to the General Assembly of Virginia. The folks in our section of Fincastle County east of Kentucky sent a petition to the General Assembly asking that our section be divided into two separate distinct counties. Thomas Jefferson was the chairman of the committee to which the petition was presented.

On 6 August 1775 we were told that Thomas Burke had been appointed overseer of the poor in Montgomery County. When I did a little more checking I found that he had also been appointed as overseer of the roads in Fincastle County back in March.

Then in October I was to be told that Thomas had also been commissioned a captain of the Fincastle Militia by the Committee of Safety. He was getting to be of great importance to our part of the state.

Also in 1775, that rascal Daniel Boone blazed a trail for the Transylvania Company from Fort Chiswell through the Cumberland Gap. It was later lengthened, following Indian trails, to reach the Falls of the Ohio River near Louisville. The Wilderness Road was steep, rough and narrow, and could only be traversed on foot or horseback. It was meant to help settlers on their way into Kentucky, but it had its problems. A more northern route called the Cumberland Road proved more efficient.

In spite of initial opposition, the General Assembly approved the petition on 7 December 1776 and Fincastle was divided into three counties. From west to east they were named Kentucky, Washington and Montgomery. John was named as one of the justices for Montgomery County. Our county was named for General Richard Montgomery. I will tell you more about him later.

Fincastle County had extended from the Blue Ridge to the Ohio River, and had an area of 12,000 square miles. Now that we were in a smaller county, we could know our neighbors better and work together for the good of us all.

Divisions of Fincastle County, 1776

Major General Richard Montgomery, 1775

But now I need to get back to the main story.

Chapter Sixteen

I was kept up to date by John and Agnes who were receiving The Virginia Gazette regularly by this time (albeit late) and fully understood why the First Continental Congress drafted a Petition to the King and organized a boycott of British goods.

The Second Continental Congress had convened on 10 May of '75. In June, after they appointed George Washington to create the Continental Army he was to oversee the capture of Boston.

On 17 June, the Army dug in on the high ground on Breed's Hill in Boston and was attacked by a frontal assault of British soldiers which surged up the hill. I took notes from an article in the newspaper I got from Agnes which said that the Patriots were ordered to hold their fire "until they could see the whites of their eyes."

Then when the regulars were close enough, our soldiers let loose with all fury a deadly barrage of musket fire. This was repeated a bit later, with no change of results. Then the third attack succeeded because our Patriots ran out of ammunition. Though the British took the hill, thousands of their soldiers' lives were lost. According to reports, we only had about 400 casualties. But among them was one of our best, General Joseph Warren. Warren had been the general who enlisted Paul Revere and William Dawes back that April to spread the alarm that the British garrison in Boston was setting out to raid the town of Concord.

That, for some reason, became known as the Battle of Bunker Hill. I never quite understood why. I gather that it was likely because Bunker Hill was larger than Breed's Hill. But to me that is a little like calling Christiansburg Richmond because Richmond is bigger.

I knew what was coming after that, and what must be done. I'm so glad Agnes shared her newspapers with me!

I also need to mention here that on 26 July '75, while the Second Continental Congress was still in session, Benjamin Franklin, the publisher of Poor Richard's Almanack which impressed me, oversaw the creation of the United States Postal Service. Still it did not go into full operation for a long time, but the door had been opened!

The British were not totally driven out of Boston until March of '76.

Colonel Henry Knox had had the foresight to transport an enormous amount of captured military supplies, including more than fifty cannons, from New York's Fort Ticonderoga across snowy terrain, arriving in Boston in late January. Benedict Arnold had aided Ethan Allen and his Green Mountain Boys in seizing them when they captured the fort on 10 May '75. Canons were placed in fortifications around the city early in the month and used to bombard the British for two straight days. On the night of the 4th, I read, several thousand of Washington's men and more of the canons were placed in position at Dorchester Heights, overlooking Boston and the harbor. General Howe realized that his troops couldn't defend the town against the Continental Army any longer. On the 17th, after eight years of occupation, Howe ordered the evacuation of Boston, hastily leaving, and sailed without incident to Nova Scotia, Canada, which was a British colony.

I was so delighted at this news that I made a nice pudding for my family to celebrate.

Yes, I was very thankful that I was getting the newspapers from Agnes. Having such a dear friend who was so kind and understood me so well was a real blessing.

On 3 July that year, at Cambridge, Washington took command of the entire Continental Army, around 17,000 men.

Then on 23 August, Sir William Howe, the British commander, launched a counter offensive and captured New York in the Battle of Brooklyn.

After the Patriots sent their "Olive Branch Petition" to the King and Parliament two days later, both of whom rejected it, the Continental Army invaded British Quebec. That didn't go well at all.

Hostilities began to rise in Virginia the very next month and the Patriots went up against Governor Dunmore who refused to abandon what he viewed as his colony without a fight. The militia in Williamsburg seized a British ship that had run aground near Hampton in a hurricane. Initially they captured the crew, but soon released them. This was the first Revolutionary action in the South. Dunmore called for a blockade around Hampton Roads and began fortification of Norfolk, a loyalist stronghold. The Patriot Safety Committee authorized nine regiments to be raised in defense of Virginia. Captain Thomas Burke headed one of these, and became an important man in this awful war.

I tore the front page off of the August 26th issue of the Virginia Gazette that Agnes let me have after they were through reading it. It reported stories from both London and Philadelphia about the war. No one wanted it, but both sides were determined to win.

Virginia Gazette, **August 25, 1775**

Chapter Seventeen

After months of raids and skirmishes, Virginia's first major battle took place at Great Bridge, south of Norfolk. Colonel John Woodford, commander of the Virginia troops, won a victory there and proclaimed it "a second Bunker Hill." To him, the tide was being reversed.

Then in late November, according to my notes, the 28th, the American Navy was established by Congress. We were becoming a force to be reckoned with on the world scene. The very next day, Congress formed a committee to seek help from possible allies in Europe who were not happy with Britain and how they were treating us. That proved later to be a very wise move.

Another expedition to Quebec under Benedict Arnold started from Cambridge, Massachusetts at year's end and ended in tragedy. Our Virginia General, Richard Montgomery, was killed at what is called "The Battle of Quebec" on 31 December.

In spite of everything, George still remained adamant in his loyalty to the Crown. He continued to view our success upon the generosity of the King. He never seemed to realize that Great Britain was supposedly being governed, to some extent, by Prime Ministers, and that the current one was Charles Watson-Wentworth, 2nd Marquess of Rockingham, who was in opposition to the Crown. Strangely enough, Lord Rockingham, the newspaper had reported, was a keen supporter of constitutional rights for the colonists.

On the 4th of July, 1776, Congress unanimously approved the Declaration of Independence that had been drafted by Thomas Jefferson in June and presented to them two days earlier. It was finally signed on August 2nd. The militia was then taken over by the Revolutionary forces. That changed everything!

Dunmore soon evacuated Virginia. After that, things got even worse. The Declaration of Independence was sent to Great Britain in November but the Crown was by no means giving up!

The Continental Congress formed the Virginia Line, or quota of infantry regiments assigned to Virginia. George Washington was given temporary control over certain military decisions or "dictatorial powers" on 27 December 1776.

Early in '77 he offered command of one of these regiments to Nathanial Gist and another to William Grayson, both of Virginia. Later he offered a third command to another fellow Virginian, Charles Thurston.

On 5 May 1777, "An Act for regulating and disciplining the Militia" was passed by the General Assembly in order to better organize and train the Virginia Colony's Militia during the Revolution.

Col. George Washington, Va. Militia, 1772

Beginning on 5 September 1777, the First Continental Artillery Regiment began to be organized in Williamsburg. Patriots were revolting. Shortly after, infantry regiments were formed, including one in our county.

John Montgomery, who was already a captain in the Virginia Militia, was naturally allowed to retain this rank in the Continental Army.

As an officer, John was given confidential information about covert military operations. Agnes later confided in me about a very close secret. I had to swear that I would not tell a soul. I was so glad that Agnes trusted me so much. John had told her on his first furlough that Washington had created a group of spies around New York, particularly on Long Island, in Setauket and the Oyster Bay area, which was called the Culper Ring. Of course he was not permitted to reveal to anyone, even Agnes, the names of the spies.

Michael was eager to serve. Rather than being placed in our neighbor's regiment, however, he was to be in the command of Captain James Finley and later also served under a Captain Thomas Ingles. I somehow got the feeling that John had chosen not to take him because of the close bonds with our family.

James would have joined also, as he was of age, but he was excused because of his frail physical condition.

Needless to say, I couldn't convince my Tory husband to fight for the freedom of the colonies from the mother country. But by that time it wasn't an option. The same provisions applied as had always been in the militia. All free males between 16 and 50 must now serve, if able. Our neighbors were all doing so and I was getting quite embarrassed.

On 11 September 1780, I had Agnes Montgomery come over to watch our children, harnessed up our new horse, Carrie, an English Running Horse, to the buggy we now owned and drove a stubborn George to Fort Chiswell to volunteer for service.

Jake and Sugar had gotten very old and were spending most of their time out in the pasture. I had already contacted a horse farm to pick them up. I hated so much to see them go. They had been so important to us, but I didn't want the children to watch them die.

That day George marked his X on an Oath of Allegiance to the Commonwealth of Virginia, stating that he would not ever take part in any treasonous or traitorous conspiracies formed against Virginia or any other of the United States of America. What was the most humiliating part was that John Montgomery was the officer to whom he submitted the Oath.

Just after George had signed up for service to Virginia, Shep drug in from the woods one day after an apparent squirrel chase (I never convinced that dear canine that he was a stock dog instead of a hunting hound). He lay down by the front porch, stretched out and just stayed there. James tried to feed him, but he seemed to have no interest in eating. Then James asked me if he could stay outside with him that night, but I insisted that he go in to bed. I counted the years and Shep was over 17. I knew that he was just plain worn out.

The next morning we found Shep under the porch. We buried him beneath a tree on the hill behind the barn. We all cried.

On 30 October, George was missing from duty. A few days later I was standing by the majestic chestnut tree next to the barn when John rode slowly up on his graceful white Thoroughbred

stallion in full uniform. I gazed upward into his saddened face as he leaned down to tell me the bad news and ask me if I had seen him. He didn't want James to hear me, as he wasn't too far away.

John's words pierced deep into my soul. All of George's statements about the King and how much he had done for us went over and over like ripples of rushing water throughout my being. My anger began building. This was not good. He certainly had not come home. I hated to admit it but I couldn't help but believe that my worst fears had likely come to pass.

Chapter Eighteen

In April, after lengthy surveillance of British troops, a brave lieutenant in the Continental Army snuck into the enemy camp one night and captured George. I was told that George at once admitted that he had deserted on a march to Smithfield, Virginia. He was quite naturally imprisoned and immediately fined two months pay.

Capture at Winchester, Virginia Militia

I was so angry that I never wanted to see him again! Young Georgie, now eleven, like James, felt my utter frustration. I had to let him know what had happened.

"What did Papa get arrested for, Mama?" he said in a trembling voice.

"They call it treason, son!"

Curses were in my head, but I dared not let them out with my children nearby. *Damn him! Why did he not listen to me? Why did he do this ungodly thing?*

But all I said was, "I will never forgive him!"

Even in the simple statement I made, my tone and words were harsh, I know. But I loved our new country and I would have been willing to defend it with my own life. Being from Holland, I had shifted loyalties as a child in order to better myself and have a brighter future. I had listened to my papa and mama! George had always been a loyalist, and I reckoned he always would be. I couldn't live with that, and I wouldn't.

I learned that he had been only one of many in the Virginia Colony to rebel as Tories, a great number of whom were from Montgomery County. They had even formed their own militia.

In fact, I found out that on 18 July 1779, Colonel William Preston (a former member of the House of Burgesses and signer of the Fincastle Resolutions) wrote a letter to Thomas Jefferson, then Governor of Virginia, stating that he had received intelligence that a number of Tories had "embodied themselves up New River in this county [Montgomery County, Virginia], that they took Prisoners; Captains Cox, Osborn & Henderson, the former of whom made his escape. That they also took two men who were sent as spies and kept them...... Prisoners in which time the spies heard them say that they intended to take the Lead Mines & that they had but 105 men there they made were five hundred strong...."

Those lead mines were the Patriots' only supply of lead for ammunition.

He further stated that this situation had greatly alarmed the people in the area. Captain William Campbell, a brother-in-law of Governor Patrick Henry, he explained, was waiting at the mines with forty-eight men for militia reinforcement to come. He was hoping that he could be allowed to bring the situation under control without further government assistance.

Jefferson wrote back to Preston on 7 August, giving him the authority, under an act already passed, to raise enough men in the county to join them to take complete charge of the defense of the Commonwealth and appoint officers to command them. He was to "report back to the Executive in Williamsburg."

Colonel Preston was able to raise the men needed and the Tories were soundly defeated. Some of the Tories were hanged, others arrested.

About 300 political prisoners were housed in the Public Gaol in Williamsburg alone between 1777 and 1780.

Colonel William Preston

In '80, Captain William Campbell was promoted to Colonel and was one of nine militia commanders who led in the decisive Patriot victory at King's Mountain, North Carolina.

British Major Patrick Ferguson had been sent to South Carolina in early September to recruit troops for the Loyalist militia to protect the flank of Lord Cornwallis' main forces. After learning of an oncoming Patriot attack, on 7 October, Ferguson retreated to the safety of Lord Cornwallis' army. The Patriots caught up with the loyalists just across the state line at King's Mountain and Ferguson was mortally wounded while trying to break the Patriot line. That battle was described in the newspaper as being "the war's largest all-American fight." I can say with all certainty that it was instrumental in winning the war.

After two years in gaol in Augusta County, in August 1780 George was taken before a military tribunal to be court-martialed for treason against the state. Upon his confession, rather than receive thirty-nine lashes, he was given the privilege of enlisting in the Continental Army directly under Washington and serving eighteen months after arrival at his camp. His enlistment began on 11 September, our thirty-first wedding anniversary! What a slap in my face that was!

He asked to see me, sending word by Captain John Montgomery. My answer was an absolute no and I was growing more bitter each day.

Young George and John, now in their teens, were certainly capable of tending and managing the farm without their father's assistance. They had already been doing a lot of the work: clearing, planning, harvesting and hanging the tobacco up to dry in the barn that they had prepared the first year it was grown. I would have no slaves, for I was adamantly opposed to it. The horror of coming to America aboard the *Molly*, hearing the pitiful cries of those wrongfully imprisoned, smelling the stench of human waste and sweat; realizing the lack of basic human rights they received had made me totally abhorrent of it.

Chapter Nineteen

During the time George was in gaol I had a lot of time to think. Never before had I felt so debased and used. Even worse than sailing over the ocean on that dang slave ship! George had seemed so truly dedicated to me when we were young. He had worked hard to provide a home and feed his family. I knew he loved our children. But what would make a man care more for a king and the way of his previous land than his family and the future that we could have had together here in America?

I would spend a lot of time with Agnes and unburden my soul on her. I hope she didn't mind so much. I know she was sympathetic to my plight. But I longed to have both a truly romantic and patriotic bond like she had with John. I let my thoughts wander to what ifs. I just had to keep myself from losing my sanity. Agnes always had an open door and an intent ear. I was thankful. And I always loved it when John was able to spend time at home, which wasn't very often then. I hope he didn't see how I looked at him, and even more so, I hope Agnes didn't. At least I had enough common sense to leave them alone after John had brought me up to date on what was going on with the government and the war. He knew how much that meant to me and always spent the time selflessly to appease my curiosity.

In his first battle, George was with Washington on 21 September '80 when Benedict Arnold betrayed him, defecting to the British side. His name became a byword for betrayal. I hope that made George realize how fortunate he was to be privileged to serve in the Continental Army.

George was also with Washington at Yorktown when he secured the amazing victory on 19 October 1781.

But before George was released, something horrible took place.

I will start with what else was going on that led up to it. Governor Thomas Jefferson, in '81, stated that the roads in Virginia were under the government of the county courts, subject to be controlled by the general court. He stated that the residents were divided into precincts by these roads.

This establishment and maintenance was one of the most important functions of the courts.

Beginning back in '77, roads had been created all over Montgomery County, and local men were appointed by the court to care for them and see that they are kept in repair. Some of those so appointed were John Heavin, John Wylie, James McCorkle, John Middleton and Charles Blakey.

It was this type of progress that made our area continue to grow. Several ferries were ordered over New River to make it easy to travel one side of the county to the other. Ingles' Ferry was most handy for me. It has been there since '62, though. I found out when I first used the ferry that it was run by Colonel William Ingles, who was the husband of Mary Draper Ingles, the lady who had been captured by Shawnee back in July '55, and managed to escape three months later.

Mary Draper Ingles

On a bitter cold day January of '82 I was taking James in the buggy to the only doctor within forty miles, at Fort Chiswell. There was a tavern standing by the river near where the ferry was docked. My breath was making white puffs in the cold stillness of the winter air as I handed Colonel Ingles the reigns. As we slowly eased across the river I asked him to tell me more about what had happened to his Mary. He was brief and evasive. I knew he didn't want to talk about that terrible time. Now that I had seen him, I wanted to meet Mary as well and hear more about her harrowing adventure directly from her. But I couldn't think of exposing her to James, especially after what she had been through. I knew there would be another time to see her. What a tough woman she had to be!

What happened with James on that trip and afterward is my next heartbreaking story.

Ingles Ferry

Michael, as I said, was away at war. James, who had always been sickly, had become very ill with influenza in February. The doctor at Fort Chiswell told me that I could only hope to make him more comfortable. He said that I must keep him in a room to himself, in bed. He told me to check on him often and make sure that he had enough to eat and drink—particularly enough water.

On the first day of March, my dear James went to meet his Maker. We buried him on the knoll where Barbara and Elizabeth had been laid to rest. It was, of course, another very gloomy time for me, and the other children took it awfully hard. I made sure that Uncle Sam and his family were notified, and they were there to mourn with me at his burial. Sammy, particularly, was genuinely broken up because he had gotten to know James when he was working here, and had come here to visit James a couple of times. They had a lot in common, though James was younger. For one thing, they both enjoyed playing checkers and Sammy would bring his set when he came.

Every time we lost a family member I had a bad battle with depression, but I knew that I must be strong for my other boys.

Chapter Twenty

I had William, who was very near his sixteenth birthday, saddle Carrie and ride to Fort Chiswell. I instructed him to tell the officer in charge to let George know about the passing of our dear son as soon as he reported in. I knew that he had to be cleared there before he could attempt to come home. He would surely be heartbroken, and I dreaded the time when he would be back. That day was rapidly closing in on me.

On Monday, 11 March, George's service time was over. It was three weeks later, on Monday the 25th, when he came banging on my door. At once, I sent the boys into a bedroom and barred both front doors—one entered the living area, the other, my bedroom. The back door stayed heavily latched all the time.

"Me love, it's George, I'm home! Open the door!" he said in a louder tone than I had ever heard him use.

"No! What you did is unforgivable!" I exclaimed.

"Oh, me love! You can't mean that! I got yer message about our dear James! I need to talk to you!"

"There is nothing left for us to talk about, George! I'm in the process of divorcing you and our children are going by my maiden name!"

Their names had not been legally changed, but that was part of my plan to make sure George knew, without a doubt, that it was over for our marriage.

I could plainly hear his muffled crying. I knew that he had looked forward with all of his heart to having a prosperous plantation.

"When you chose the King over me, you made your bed, now you must lie in it!" I said sternly.

"I've never stopped lovin' ya, Christy, darlin'! We belong together!"

"The children want nothing to do with you!"

The boys stayed out of sight and said not a word. They knew they mustn't.

George was beside himself.

"Think what ye're a doin', Christy! Please let me in!

"Now you know I'm not going to do that, George! Go away and never come back!"

"I'll be in touch with ya!" he yelled.

George knew that I meant business. In a few minutes I watched through the window as he walked slowly away and faded into the distance, up the road toward town.

Chapter Twenty-one

Not long after George's visit I was awakened shortly after falling asleep one night by the high-pitched squawking of the chickens and the harsh barking of Shep! I grabbed my gun and headed out to the hen house. Obviously the combined sounds of Shep's course voice and my opening and closing the front door of the house caused enough ruckus that the pesky invader skedaddled. I saw a flash of reddish fur and a bushy white-tipped tail hightailing it out toward the woods to the south. I could not have foxes invading our livelihood! We had managed to keep the hawks from catching them, mostly because someone was outside a lot during the daylight hours and I guess they got tired of waiting till no one was around.

All was still for a few nights and the incident was repeated. This time, sadly, one of the hens fell prey to the enemy. I nicknamed the fox "George."

It was happening about ten-thirty at night according to the clock on the fireplace mantle. I decided I would take the loaded gun, wrap up good, and lie in wait on the porch until he showed his furry face again.

Three nights later, I saw "George" creeping toward the hen house, aimed carefully and ended our problem. Shep was on him like a duck on a June bug, but he was too late. He shook and shook that poor dead fox till I had to forcibly take it away from him. He didn't like it, but I had no way to know if the little fella was diseased, so I put him in a wooden box and buried him the next day.

After I felt certain that George had accepted what I had done, and that he wasn't coming back to haunt me, I just felt like I needed to clear my head. He had tried to get to me through John, but he found that didn't work either.

It was a cool early morning toward the end of April and a late frost lay lightly on the meadow. I quickly saddled Carrie and jumped on, side-saddle. My long skirt, hanging loosely on the left, was soon blowing in the soft breeze created by Carrie's graceful motion as we bounded through the field of Timothy, the stubble field of wheat, and into the woods to our west. I had ridden about a mile and a half, I reckoned, and was in a rolling hillside meadow when lo; just ahead of me, near the edge of a dense pine thicket, I witnessed a most gallant spectacle! Two stately elk were peacefully grazing. The bull, edging close to the cow, raised his head ever so slowly and looked down at me as if to welcome me to his abode. His breath was freezing and his antlers looked like wooden coat racks against the deep green pine needles. The cow merely glanced up; then continued grazing.

Carrie was halted, motionlessly staring in their direction.

I wondered why they didn't dash away into the safety of the woods. Carrie lifted her beautiful head and whinnied. The bull opened up with the most unique cry. It sounded a bit like a bugle. It began low and gradually became a loud scream. I later learned that this is a mating call and a warning to other bulls to stay away from him. What a sound! What a sight to behold!

Then the bull began a sequence that seemed like a chuckle or a laugh. Carrie and I just stayed glued to the ground for several minutes before those beautiful creatures slowly ambled away into the woods. I shall never forget that glorious experience.

Even though deer were common on our farm, this was a lot different. I had never before or since witnessed the presence of elk in the wild. It was breathtaking.

This was just the thing that I needed to remind me of the beauty of life amongst the thorns that prick us. I pulled the reign to the right, said "gee," and turned Carrie around to head toward home.

On the way I noticed only the good that was all around me. The melting frost announcing the arrival of morning. The brightness and grandeur of the rising sun over the mountain peaks back beyond my wonderful home. I pulled my bonnet down to shade my eyes, but soon fluffy clouds rode in on the breeze to oblige my need as I moved slowly onward.

My thoughts and attitude were now on a solid hope for tomorrow and the positive future that I was conjuring up in the deep recesses of my oft muddled mind.

A young hare dashed across in front of us as we victoriously entered our meadow. I was home, where God had placed me. I was happy; I was free.

Chapter Twenty-two

After the war ended in September of '83 and Michael came home he told me some amazing stories of all the events that had happened in the war that even John didn't know about. As usual, I wrote everything down.

He had been wounded once, but it was not a serious injury, just grazing his shoulder at Stony Point, New York, under the command of "Mad Anthony" Wayne.

But even more interesting to me, though mostly sad, was his relating of the Battle of Brandywine Creek on 11 September '77, the first conflict in which he had taken part, where Washington went up against Sir William Howe.

One thing greatly interested me that he told me of his experiences there besides the actual battle. He had met another young local man, Jacob Allen Albert, a hero who fought by his side.

Albert had gained fame during the war, serving as a scout to the German speaking area of

Pennsylvania, gathering information on Tory sympathizers and locating the position of British troops. It was a very dangerous detail, and he knew that Nathan Hale had been captured doing the very same thing a year earlier and put to death. He told Michael that he had received a pay of only six pounds for the ten week term of duty. Michael didn't use the word "only," but that is how I felt about it.

Howe moved in to take Philadelphia which was still our Capitol at the time. The regulars routed the Continental Army, forcing them to withdraw to Chester, Pennsylvania; then in a northeasterly direction toward Philadelphia. More troops fought in that battle, he told me, than any other battle in the war, even the ones before he was serving. It was also the longest battle, with a full eleven hours of continuous fighting.

Howe's army, Michael said, had marched in from Sandy Hook, New Jersey across the bay from New York City, at the tip of Manhattan Island. The city was already occupied by the British, as I mentioned earlier.

On 23 July they had landed at the point of the Head of the Elk by the Elk River at the northern end of Chesapeake Bay. On their march north, the British had skirmishes, he had been informed, with light factions of our army.

Michael was with Washington when he offered battle with his forces posted behind Brandywine Creek off the Christina River. While some were involved in front of Chadd's Ford, Howe took the bulk of his troops on a long march that crossed Brandywine far beyond Washington's right flank.

Due to poor scouting, the Continental Army failed to detect Howe's column until it reached the rear of their flank.

Late in doing so, three divisions were shifted to block the British flanking forces at the Quaker Birmingham Friends Meetinghouse and School.

After a hard fight, Howe's wing broke through the American right wing which was deployed on several hills.

It was then that Lieutenant General Wilhelm von Knyphausen, fighting with Britain, attacked Chadd's Ford and crumpled the American left wing. As Washington's army streamed away in retreat, he brought in parts of Nathanael Greene's division and was able to hold off Howe's column long enough for his army to escape to the northeast.

Washington kept a positive attitude and in his detailed report to the Continental Congress he stated, "Despite the day's misfortune, I am pleased to announce most of my men are in good spirits and still have the courage to fight the enemy another day."

After that conflict, in October, another Virginia regiment, commanded by Nathaniel Greene, held the British at Germantown while Washington withdrew the rest of his men, including my Michael's unit, to save the Continental Army from certain disaster.

On 30 November, Michael said, Washington settled on Valley Forge, about 20 miles northwest of Philadelphia, as the most suitable place for winter quarters.

Washington at Valley Forge

Chapter Twenty-three

The Continental Congress had been forced to abandon Philadelphia on 12 December 1776, which I already knew. First they moved to Lancaster, but for only one day; then to York, Pennsylvania. Military supplies were moved to Reading, Pennsylvania.

The embarrassing defeat at Brandywine Creek left Philadelphia vulnerable. The British captured it two weeks later on 26 September and it was under British control for almost nine months.

During the time of occupation, the Continental Army froze and suffered appalling deprivation at Valley Forge. However, capable European strategists contacted by our young government, including Prussian Baron von Stuben, French Marquis de Lafayette and several others, sided with the Patriots and aided Washington in creating a well-drilled professional force to help them defeat the British.

I later read an article in The Virginia Gazette published in Williamsburg that quoted a man in

Lafayette's company talking about his journey from Charleston, South Carolina to Philadelphia which was taken in a carriage caravan. I wrote these lines down from the article:

"The carriage was a sort of uncovered sofa upon four springs, with a forecarriage. At the side of this carriage he had one of his servants on horseback, who acted as his squire." The article went on to say that his two counselors, colonels, "followed in a second carriage with two wheels." Four days later, said the man, "some of our carriages were reduced to splinters, several of the horses which were old and unsteady, were either worn out or lame, and we were obliged to buy others along the road... We reached a great part of the way on foot, often sleeping in the woods, almost dead from hunger, exhausted with heat..."

Lafayette's true dedication to the cause of our fledgling country showed me how truly he sympathized with our cause. His trip seems more than merely heroic.

On 18 June 1778, 15,000 British troops under Sir Henry Clinton evacuated Philadelphia and the Continental Congress was returned there.

Michael told me that his father had served in the same battles as he, much of the time, and wanted desperately to have a relationship with him. He said that at first he had barely been civil to him, and had told him plainly that he fully sided with me.

As time went on, Michael softened. He told me that he simply could not hold a grudge any longer and had made peace with George, telling him that he had forgiven him.

They had served in different regiments, but both had been in the forces at the decisive victory of the Siege of Yorktown in the fall of '81. There had only been a small force of about 2,500 Americans left in New York.

There, Washington had been bravely aided by the French allies, like Lafayette and the French Army led by Comte de Rothambeau, who commanded 4,000 French troops.

The British were led by Cornwallis, who surrendered on 19 October, leading to the eventual culmination of the war. Michael and his father had both fought with this band of brave troops.

In addition to the main siege led by the French, Colonel Alexander Hamilton, Michael said, had led a separate siege there with a small band of infantrymen. Hamilton had made it clear that he wanted to improve his image in battle, as he had not done well before. He was fortunate enough to talk Washington into it.

The French troops were given the attack on redout Number 9. Hamilton was assigned redout Number 10. Washington ordered the use of bayonets rather than "pounding them slowly into submission with the cannon."

That night the sky lit up as the allies fired a number of shells into the air.

Michael could see Hamilton and his men rally from the trenches, dashing across a quarter mile field with fixed bayonets. They had unloaded their guns in order to use bayonets alone. Silence and surprise won out. Dodging heavy fire they let out war whoops and startled the enemy!

It had taken less than ten minutes, and proved effective. Hamilton lost only 27 of his 400 infantrymen! Hamilton had redeemed himself and helped make the total siege a huge success.

Michael also told me that the Culper Group of spies that Washington had organized were also a great help in winning the war. After the war ended they no longer needed secrecy. He told me that it had been headed by a young cavalry officer named Benjamin Tallmadge in his hometown of Setauket, Long Island. The people he recruited were his most trusted friends. The first persons he chose were a farmer named Abraham Woodhull and Caleb Brewster, who commanded of a fleet of whaleboats against Tory and British shipping on Long Island Sound. Tallmadge used the code name John Bolton, and Woodhull went by Samuel Culper. This is how the group got its name. In '79, he told me, Tallmadge had recruited a well-connected New York merchant named Robert Townsend, who took the name Samuel Culper, Junior.

They had carried messages across Long Island Sound letting Washington know about the intentions of the regulars. It had become the most effective of any intelligence gathering operation on either side during the war. They had even identified the treason of Benedict Arnold plotting with British Major John Andre to turn over West Point and surrender the fort to the British forces!

I had never told him, of course, that I had been aware of this operation almost from the beginning.

Right after that, I talked with Agnes again about it and she told me that one of the most important members of the ring, known at the time as Agent 355, had actually been a woman named Anna Strong! Well bully for her! Other women were also involved, she said. Now that it was all over, these brave women could be given credit. It made me so very proud! This got me more interested than ever. These women were as much heroes as the men.

I determined right then that I must meet Anna Strong.

On 15 February 1780 John was finally rewarded with a land grant near his other property for 3,000 acres for service to the Crown and the Colony during the French and Indian Wars. It seemed strange to me that they would still reward him after he had fought in the

Continental Army against them. Actually, it was the fulfillment of a promise made at the time of service, and the Crown didn't want a black mark lingering.

John was now one of the wealthiest men in our county. But this is not why I was proud that he was our friend. It was because of his bravery and desire for doing what was right; that and the enduring friendship I had with his darling wife.

Michael enlarged our house once again. At least he had inherited his father's building skills. A huge front room was added from lumber purchased in the village. Other bedrooms were added.

In the back of my mind I had plans for that house. Michael soon started courting a fine young lady from our thriving community.

In 1781 I heard about another remarkable female spy. Her name was Nancy Ann Morgan Hart. I heard of her first from Agnes, who had of course, been told her story by John.

She reportedly had been born in rural North Carolina, not that far south of us. She was a

151

cousin to American General Daniel Morgan. She had married Benjamin Hart and borne him eight children, Agnes said. Sometime in the '70s, the story went, they had moved first to South Carolina, then to the Broad River Region in the Mountains of northeast Georgia. There Nancy took well to the frontier lifestyle. She was a very imposing figure, I was told; over six feet tall and red headed, with quite a temper to match. John had heard much about her. She made friends well among the Cherokees who had great respect for her. They called her, "Wahatche," meaning war woman.

She became a staunch defender of the Patriot cause. What she lacked in education, Nancy made up for in grit and the skills of survival. Her husband had joined the Georgia Militia, and while he was away at war, her abilities as an herbalist, hunter and markswoman proved imperative in protecting her family and community.

As the Revolution moved south, she played an important role in fighting against the Tories. Disguising herself as a crazy man, she wandered in and out of British encampments gathering information for the Patriots. But there were so many stories, that I wanted to also meet her and hear it from her own mouth.

Not long after the additions on my house were finished, in the summer of 1784, Michael and Catherine Creager were married. I allotted him a section of fifty acres on the southwest end of our farm. He began his house there, and soon had six head of cattle and six horses, including two Quarter Horses from Janus's line.

I went to court and the divorce was finalized. On 15 April 1785 I was granted the entire 344 acres, so I had it surveyed. A new deed was drawn up in my name and those of my younger sons, John, George, William and Jacob.

The road on which our home stood ran along the creek between the Montgomery's and my land, to the southwest and was now a continuation of The Great Road. It would be an important thoroughfare for travelers coming into town from both the north and the southwest.

There was nothing else George could do.

Chapter Twenty-four

On 5 March 1787, one of Michael's neighbors, George Irwin, sold him 29 more acres on Reed Creek, adjoining the acreage he already had, for fifty pounds. He had finished his house two years earlier, and would now have a nice sized little farm.

In July of '87 my mind ran back on the events when James was sick and I remembered how very much I had wanted to meet the daring Mary Ingles. She and I had to be a lot alike. We had both been to hell and back and kept going. It wasn't but a few miles, so one day I asked young George to stay home and take care of the children while I rode up to Ingles Ferry. I saddled up Carrie and we rode like the wind over the wagon road and made it in less than an hour. Mary was sitting on the porch of the tavern. There was a smoky fog hanging low on the river. She was a solemn, yet lovely lady, appearing to be in her fifties at the time. I dismounted and grasped the reigns tightly as I looked over at her.

"Hello, Mary," I said. "I'm Christiana Crewey. I live over in Hans Meadows. I was born in Holland and my husband and I came here from England. I've been through a lot of struggles. I've long heard about your remarkable story of capture, survival and escape from the Shawnees back during the French and Indian War. I greatly admire your bravery. I wanted to hear your story straight from you."

"Come on up here and sit with me," she said, pointing to a rocker beside her. It was a slow day for the ferry which she had been running alone. "What do you want to know?"

I tied Carrie's reigns to the rail next to the water trough on the left of the building.

"There have been so many different tales told," I said, "I want you to start from the beginning and tell me what really happened."

"I appreciate your interest, Christiana. Did you know that I lost my Will about five years ago?"

"No," I said, "I'm so sorry. I met him in January of '82 when I crossed the river on the ferry. He must have passed not long after I met him."

"Thank you. Yeah, it was in '82, all right. Did you know that he was one of the signers of the

Fincastle Resolutions? Can't bring him back but I sure do miss him!"

"I know you do! And he was a true hero as well! I do remember reading his name, but didn't know that was your husband!

"I don't miss mine! He's not dead, but he's out of my life. I sure miss my younguns that have passed on, though."

"Well, I'll tell you everything. It's a long story, so I hope you can stay with me for a spell."

"No problem, Mary. I will stay as long as it takes."

"Wonderful! It's lonely here when I ain't got any guests and I can use the company. My family came to Philadelphia from Ireland, then on down here to Virginia to farm. My parents were the first white settlers in these mountains. After my papa's disappearance my family and a fella named James Burke settled over yonder at what people started calling Draper Meadows. I met Will and we got married. I was just 18 and he was 21. It was the first white wedding in this part of the country, I was told. We had two boys. Our Thomas was the first white boy born west of the Alleghenies.

"After the war started with the French we didn't think we had any fear from the Indians. Folks around there felt safe 'cause the Indians in these parts were peaceful, and we had no idea that the Shawnees, who were fighting on the side of the French, would ever come around our place.

"On the 8th day of July in '55, a savage bunch of Shawnee attacked us. Six of us were killed including my mama, my brother's gal, and Colonel James Patton who had been pursuing the Indians and tried to help us. I'd seen him before, so I knew who he was. Me and my two sons, Thomas and George; my sister-in-law, Bettie, and our neighbor, Henry Leonard, were all captured. I guess that's because we didn't try to fight back. We ran and hid in our houses. Will was in the field and came a running in when he heard all the commotion. They hurt Will pretty bad, but he got away by running into the woods."

"That was awful, I'm so sorry!" I said, frowning.

"The Indians took several of our horses and raided our houses, packing our belongings onto the horses." She continued. "Then they forced us to walk along the banks of the rivers many hundreds of miles into Kentucky.

It took us a full month to get to Lower Shawnee-town. Before we arrived, they made all of the others run the gauntlet between two rows of their warriors who hit them with sticks."

"I can't imagine that!"

"I alone wasn't made to do that. It could have been because I was with child. One of the braves wanted to save me for himself. He didn't seem to care that I was carrying a baby inside of me. He took me and used me as his squaw. It made me so dang mad! Every time he forced himself on me I jest screamed and screamed. I could hear the other braves laughing from their tents.

I could see tears trailing down her pale cheeks. I was gritting my teeth and shaking my head. What horror she had endured! But that wasn't nearly all of it.

Captive running the gauntlet

Chapter Twenty-five

She kept on with her story.

"Both of my boys were taken from me and sent to other places to be adopted by Shawnee families. In less than a month I gave birth to my sweet little girl. I named her Bettie Eleanor for my sister-in-law.

"It wasn't long till my neighbor, Henry, managed to escape. That gave me a little hope, but they watched us even closer after that.

"While I was there I saw a goodly number of white pioneers who had also been taken captive in Virginia. They kept us from talking with 'em, so I don't know where they were taken from. They looked to be English or Irish; and I heard some of 'em speaking English at a distance.

"About three weeks after arriving at Lower Shawneetown, I traveled with two of the braves about 100 miles to the southwest to a settlement called Big Bone Lick to make salt for 'em by boiling brine and serve 'em while we were there. We knew we were a lot farther from home! An old Dutch woman and I were left alone while a group of them Indians went on a hunt. After all day they hadn't got back. I saw this as my chance, and persuaded the old Dutch woman to slip into the woods with me while those in the camp were a eating supper near 'bout dark.

"We knew no other way to go toward home without passing through the Indian town, so we spent that night in a cornfield jest out a ways. We got up very early the next morning before the Shawnees waked up and went around the village without being seen.

"I hated so much having to leave my darling baby at Shawneetown, but I couldn't risk going back. I knew we'd both be facing a death sentence.

"As we traveled as quietly as possible up the Ohio River, we came very close to an Indian brave who was skinning a deer afore we seed him. We hid behind a big ole log, but the Indian's dog spotted us and started a barking. Not only did the dog scare us, but the Indian as well! He ran away, leaving the deer for us to feast on. So there was even a purpose in this. After satisfying our hunger, we took as much of the meat as we were able to carry on our journey homeward. Along the river we found grapes and nuts to eat, but still got awful' hungry again in about three weeks. About starving to death, the old Dutch woman turned on me like she was gonna try to kill me. I feared she meant to eat me. She had me firmly in her grasp and was a strangling the very life out of me!"

I was cringing. I wondered if I should have told her that I was Dutch. I couldn't help but believe that the old woman was one of the German settlers which I had heard folks call the "Pennsylvania Dutch."

"With all the strength I could muster I finally got out of her grip and ran as fast as I could in my weak condition.

"It was late November and a skiff of snow was on the ground before I came dragging in to a community near our Draper Meadows. I was only twenty-three years old, but my hair was white and my naked body was so thin that my ribs were sticking through my sides.

"I had been walking along the rivers for forty long days. I heard someone working gathering the last nubbins of corn on the freezing stalks in a cornfield.

"'Hallo,' I said as loud as my weak voice could muster. No one heard. 'Hallo! Hallo...' again I squeaked out.

"I lifted my head a bit through the stalks and could see the form of a man and two big hearty boys.

"Them three fellas reached for their guns; they knew the Shawnees couldn't be trusted and that this could be a trick. They couldn't chance another massacre.

"The next time I called out I put ever' last ounce of my strength into it. My voice, he later told me, sounded vaguely familiar.

"'Mary Ingles?' he said, is that you?

"It was Adam Harmon, with his two sons. Adam dashed to me and took my frail body in his arms. I was more dead than alive. He carried me carefully into his cabin, wrapped me in blankets, bathed my swollen feet in warm water and fed me small portions of venison and bear meat.

"When Will finally got to me he was so happy he cried like a baby."

"What an adventure! Your story will certainly live on, my dear friend," I said.

Chapter Twenty-six

"**O**ne more story you should know about," she started in again, "our son, Thomas, stayed with the Indians till '68, when Will was able to ransom him. He spoke the Shawnee tongue and had a hard time getting back to our ways. He was unhappy being away from his Indian friends. Will finally sent him to Albemarle County where he got married.

"He sent me word that he had settled in Burke's Garden on the land he had just been given by Will. The Indians called it 'Great Swamp.'"

"Wait a minute," I interrupted, "you've mentioned the name Burke twice. I have a neighbor who is Captain Thomas Burke. Any kin?"

"Yes. Same family. I know him. Met him during the Revolution. He came by to talk with me about my story and told me that James was his uncle."

"Land o' Goshen! We know the same nice fellow!"

"Yes we do. I really liked him. Now I'll get back to what I was a tellin' ya!

"Then, to beat all the confounded tarnation, right after that, on 5 April '82, Black Wolfe and his savage Shawnees raided Burke's Garden and captured Thomas' wife and three younguns and a Negro man and woman servant! They took all the booty they could carry, too.

"Thomas and another Negro slave who was working with him heard all the commotion and the cries of his family. He knew there were too many Indians to overcome, so he went for help. The Washington County Militia was mustering and being drilled by Captain Thomas Maxwell on the North Fork of the Holston River, so Maxwell took a party of fifteen to Burke's Garden to begin pursuit of the Shawnees.

"A neighbor of Thomas', Joseph Hicks and his Negro slave were the only people besides Thomas and his family. They had been on the way to see Thomas when the Indians attacked. They had gone across Brushy Mountain for help. They were able to get six or seven men to go back with them to Burke's Garden, and arrived about the same time the Maxwell party got there. They all united in pursuit of the Indians.

"It took them five days to catch up with the savages, who were camped for the night in a gap of Tug Mountain. They all agreed for Maxwell to take half of the men during the night and get in front of the Indians, and that my Thomas would stay in the rear with the balance of them. They were to attack from both sides at daybreak.

"It was mighty dark, and the ground was rough and brushy, so Maxwell's party lost their way and didn't reach the front by daylight. When the Indians began to awaken, Thomas began his attack.

"As soon as a shot was fired some of the Indians began to attack the prisoners with tomahawks. Others fought and fled. Thomas was able to grab his wife just as she was hit hard on the head with a tomahawk! She fell suddenly to the ground, covering her baby which she was holding in her arms. Then Indians tomahawked Thomas' other two children, a boy and a girl. His Negro slaves, a man and a woman escaped without injury."

My mind was on Thomas having slaves after he himself had been captured and held against his will. I wondered if it had just become a normal part of his life because of this or if this was a sort of pay back. I thought it best not to ask her what she thought.

Mary was still talking, and I dare not let my mind wander. I wanted to hear it all.

"After they left the bloody scene, the Indians came upon Thomas Maxwell and his party, and shot and killed Captain Maxwell. The soldiers gave him a proper burial there.

"Thomas' wife and infant daughter, Rhoda, lived. The remaining family members moved to Tennessee."

Mary gave me a cold dipper of water from their well and asked me to have a bite to eat and share my story with her, which I did. It was nearly dark before I headed home. The boys were worried about me, but understood

I have an exceptional memory, and that night, before I went to bed I wrote down my conversation with Mary as best as I could. It was such a special time for me and I didn't want to forget it.

Chapter Twenty-seven

Beginning on 25 May 1787 the Federal Convention was held at Philadelphia, which established the U.S. Constitution and the federal government.

Included in the delegates were James Madison of Virginia and Alexander Hamilton of New York, who made certain that this initiative did not merely revise the league of states which had previously been formed, but would create a truly new government, the United States. They elected General George Washington to be President of the Convention and preside over it.

Several broad outlines were proposed and debated, including The New Jersey Plan of William Patterson. James Madison's Virginia plan, however, was selected as the basis for the new government, which called for setting up three distinct branches of government: legislative, executive and judicial. A number of subjects were discussed regarding the powers and limitations for these branches. Subjects like slave trade and which branch should choose judges.

Things moved slowly, I learned, until mid-July, when the Connecticut Compromise was reached and a draft was written by the Committee of Detail to be approved. The final Constitution was drawn up on parchment and signed by thirty-nine of the fifty-five delegates on 17 September.

Washington had changed a lot since he was a young twenty-two-year-old envoy of the Virginia Governor. Even a casual observer to his accomplishments could tell this.

He was being hailed as the "Father of our country," and was elected by the Electoral College to be the first President of the United States, and inaugurated on 30 April 1789, taking the Oath of Office with his hand on a Masonic Bible at Federal Hall in New York City.

One of Washington's first acts was to appoint Samuel Osgood of Massachusetts as the first Postmaster General. Right away, the Post Office Department hired post riders who were pledged to take desolate roads hundreds of mile in even the most treacherous conditions to deliver the mail to post offices throughout the colonies. It wouldn't be long before we had a post office!

Washington's Inauguration, Federal Hall

Before the White House was build, Washington and his wife Martha lived in Philadelphia.

President Washington's house in Philadelphia

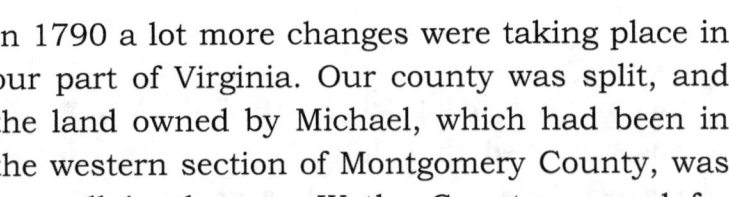

In 1790 a lot more changes were taking place in our part of Virginia. Our county was split, and the land owned by Michael, which had been in the western section of Montgomery County, was now all in the new Wythe County, named for George Wythe, the first Virginian signer of the Declaration of Independence.

But even more importantly, our town had grown to the point that Hans Meadows was the County Seat.

Chapter Twenty-eight

A meeting had been held in April of '88 in which it was "Ordered that John Montgomery, James McGavock, Walter Crockett, Andrew Boyd, and James Newell, or any three of them, agree with workmen to build a prison of logs, not less than twenty feet by eighteen feet in the clear also, a log courthouse twenty feet square in the clear with a ten foot shed at the end for a jury room, also the said committee direct the laying off of the land for the public buildings."

The '90s brought so many changes in our country, state, town and family that I hardly know where to begin.

On 1 May 1790, I attended the first court session ever held in our town which was at Hans Meadow plantation, the home of Captain James Craig, who had married John Montgomery's daughter, Anne. The main purpose was for accepting land to form the town itself.

James Craig began the offering by donating approximately 180 acres. I then deeded a strip, about fifty acres, more or less of land to the town, at the north of my farm adjoining the Hans Meadow Plantation, hoping that it would be used for the courthouse and town buildings. Samuel Kirby gave 100 acres.

I heard one of the men whispering that I was "a blue stocking." I pretended not to hear. In those days that meant "a learned woman," so I guess I ought to have felt honored. Somehow, though, at that moment, I got the feeling that some of them still didn't want women in what was considered to be men's business. At least they didn't turn my land down. I wouldn't have taken it back if they had offered. I thought about it later and decided that things were indeed changing somewhat for the better. The land I donated was very well located, so they honored me and for the most part made me feel good about myself. Everyone knew what had happened with George, and I was respected for the stand that I had taken for our independence from Britain.

The influence of the Craig family, who also owned the largest tavern in town at the time, won out and the committee voted to use the land being donated by James for the courthouse and public buildings. My land and Sam Kirby's would be cleared and divided into lots after the Craig acreage had been developed. The name of our town was left blank on the document drawn up that day.

I need to include here the fact that Thomas and Clara Burke had a daughter named for her mother. On 30 January 1790, the daughter married Jacob Snidow. Barely a year later, young Clara Snidow died in childbirth.

I took Carrie and rode up the several miles to the Burke home to express my sympathy and volunteer to help in any possible way. The house was filled with family members and I felt completely out of place, but at least I had made an effort and Clara tearfully thanked me for my concern.

In March of '91, a highway was built from the wagon ford of Tom's Creek in the north, to the newly finished courthouse. A month later a prison and stocks had been completed.

Lots were laid off, advertised in the Virginia Gazette at Williamsburg, and sold to the highest builder with the requirement that a house at least sixteen feet square must be built on each lot. My land was being used to establish the town and I was thrilled.

It didn't take long for the building lots around the center of town to sell, and the town, now called Christiansburgh, was up and going—all one-mile-square of it. Businesses began to be built and we were "in high cotton," as I have heard people from farther down south say.

I wrote down a list of the first town trustees, who were Byrd Smith, James Barnett, Hugh Crockett, Samuel Eston, Joseph Cloyd, John Preston, Christian Snidow (brother of the son-in-law of Thomas and Clara Burke), James Charlton, and of course, James Craig, Esquire.

Someone started a rumor that the town had been named for me! I don't think so! Just because I had donated a tract of land and my name was Christiana! At that time it wasn't clear for whom it was named. To this day I still have people ask me about it!

George was not hesitant to send word to me that he had remarried to a widow, Ann Hanky, on 26 October that year, here in Montgomery County. I was told later that his wife had two daughters. I couldn't have cared less except to know that he wouldn't bother me again.

Chapter Twenty-nine

Winter was fast approaching. It had been eight years since Michael came home and Agnes had told me about Anna Strong. It had been over four years since I had paid my memorable visit to Mary Ingles. Meeting and documenting the stories of the brave women heroes of the French and Indian War and Revolutionary War had now become a passion with me. I decided that I was going to New York to see Anna.

My children were grown and I need not worry about them. The balance of my farm was in capable hands with my younger sons watching over it. I explained to my boys and Agnes what I was doing. Michael would not hear of my going alone. He questioned the time of year, but told me that he had wanted to meet this brave patriotic woman since he first heard of her during the war and insisted on going with me. He knew he wasn't going to get me to wait till spring, because he was all too familiar with my determined nature. He hitched his two Quarter Horses to his phaeton for the long journey. I was delighted! I didn't want to be on the road alone, but I would have gone alone had no one volunteered. It was 3 November when he and I loaded the needed supplies onto his phaeton and we hit the Great Wagon Road headed north.

It was the first time I had been out of Virginia since we arrived there what seemed like forever ago. We didn't get out of the state for three days, camping under the skies each night. It brought back memories of my trip with George from Williamsburg so long ago.

Well, the second night it came a cold rain and we had no stars to see as the heavens above were as dark as pitch. It was already getting cold, even in the day, and we had taken heavy clothes and a lot of covers. I questioned my own decision not to wait till spring to go, but we were already well on our way. I knew I had to make this trip, and when I decided on doing something I wouldn't back out for anybody or anything.

It took us four full days just to get into Lancaster County. That was another thing I had always wanted to do—go to Lancaster where most of our neighbors, and even Uncle Sam, had once lived. At least we had a good road and great horses. I was surprised at how many Amish lived there. It seemed that the Irish and Scots Irish had mostly migrated to Virginia, but the Amish had stayed.

We met some fine folks there at shops, and bought some additional supplies for our trip on to New York.

We went from there to Philadelphia and stopped to see the Carpenter's Hall and the home that President Washington lived in. What a sight that town was!

That night we decided to stay in an inn and board the horses at the livery stable where they could be brushed and curried. I know they appreciated that. Since it was a cold night, so did we. Michael and I got a chance to talk on that trip like we hadn't in years. That alone was worth the inconveniences we faced because of the weather.

We found that it was not necessary to go into New York State before going onto Long Island, but we had to go into New Jersey. We started out early the next morning and made it to the Jersey Shore where we spent a very windy, snowy night in the phaeton at the mouth of the Hudson River. We had never imagined what a task it was just getting there across the narrow rivers. I asked myself once again if I had thought this trip through.

Early the next morning we were fortunate to find a ferry running across the Oyster Banks to the tip of the Island. There were so many people jammed into this place I could hardly believe my eyes. Once we got the phaeton on the road again, we saw that the farther we went the fewer homes and businesses we encountered. The island was huge! It just went on and on. Luckily, the roads were in good shape because of daily use, so we were able to make our way to Setauket, where we had been told that Anna and her husband, Captain Selah Strong, who had become a judge, lived. I was more than anxious to meet her and spend time in her presence.

We had asked those along the way for the exact location of the Strong home; we reached it at dusk, so I felt that we should not go calling at that late hour.

At least we knew where to go back the next morning. We found an inn with a restaurant in the town of East Setauket not more than a few blocks from their impressive dwelling. They had a livery there for our horses, and I was so glad. We had a tasty meal of fish and potatoes and got us two nice rooms with poster type beds. I was so glad that I could now afford it.

Chapter Thirty

When I arose at daybreak, I was so anxious and excited that I could hardly contain myself. I dressed and went and knocked on Michael's door to find that he was already up, dressed and ready for breakfast. After enjoying tea and a breakfast of cornmeal mush and milk, we headed to the livery to fetch our horses and hitch up the phaeton.

It was Thursday, and we arrived at the Strong home just in time to see Judge Strong stepping into his carriage to leave for court. This was a grand occurrence for we introduced ourselves, related our story and informed him of the nature of our call. He was very cordial, accompanied us to the door, repeated our story to his doorman and asked him to announce us to his wife.

Apparently the doorman had a good memory. Realizing how far we had traveled to meet her, that I was a true patriot who had even divorced my Tory husband, and that Michael had served in the Continental army, Anna greeted us with open arms.

"Please come to the parlor and sit! Would you care for a spot of tea?" she said.

Michael and I looked at one another and both shook our heads and said "No" at the same time.

"We have heard of your heroics as a member of the Culper Ring, dear lady," I said. "Women of courage fascinate me. I suppose it is because I have had to stand firm in the face of incredible circumstances. I met Mary Ingles who escaped the Indians in Kentucky. Such unbelievable strength and fortitude she had! Your story came to me in only bits. I want to hear the whole truth of it from your own mouth. Please start when you were recruited."

"Please call me Nancy," she said with a slight nod. That's what my family calls me, it's my middle name. I would like you to feel like family."

"Why, thank you." I smiled. "I am much honored! I never heard that before."

"I will start by telling you that I am the daughter of Colonel William Smith and Margaret Lloyd Smith. My husband is related to Abraham Woodhull, the one known as Samuel Culper, Senior. Selah was a delegate to three provincial congresses in New York back in '75 and '76. Then he was a Captain in the New York Militia. He was imprisoned by the British in the sugar house on 2 January '78 as a presumed spy, and was later transferred to the prison ship HMS Jersey. I took food to him both places. We had a chance to talk and he told me how badly spies were needed and that he wanted me to be available when called upon."

Michael and I were both intent on her every word, and smiling broadly.

"In early September, Abe Woodhull sent a message to me at night asking me to meet with him. I knew I must go. It was my duty to the Patriots. He lived near us, and I met with him at the farm he was using as a headquarters after dark one evening. He told me that no one would suspect my being a spy, and that I was desperately needed to keep him aware of the changes in location of another one of his spies who would be hiding.

"I agreed and my adventure began."

I was nodding and my eyes were fastened on her.

"Our home was within view of the farm and I used my laundry as a code to indicate when the information could be delivered to the next agent, Caleb Brewster.

"Caleb Brewster, Agent 725, a whaler, would be hidden in one of six local coves on the Sound and I could see them all from our house here at Strong Point. Woodhull would flash a signal to me at night. I would hang my black petticoat on my clothesline to let Brewster know that a message was ready. I would indicate to which of six coves the courier should take his boat by hanging out that number of handkerchiefs and he would meet Woodhull to pick up the message.

"Brewster took the information across the Sound on one of his whaleboats."

"I was aware of that fact, but didn't know how you accomplished this remarkable feat! I am so proud of you!"

"Thank you. I am just so glad that I was not suspected. Abe was questioned heavily at a checkpoint one day and wanted to pass a lot of his duties on to Amos Underhill, but Amos was unable to make clear reports.

"In June of '79 he was able to engage Robert Townsend, who took the code name Samuel Culper, Junior. Townsend managed to escape suspicion by authoring a society column in a Loyalist newspaper.

"I knew I must find a way to get Selah out of the prison ship, so I used the influence of Tory relatives. Yes," she smiled, "I can understand what you went through with your husband. I did have family members who were loyalists. In this case, it proved a good thing. It would likely have not worked had they had the vaguest idea that I was a spy, myself."

"Oh, my!" I said. "You do understand! Yet, like me, you stayed true to the American dream!"

"Yes, I did."

"Did everyone respect you after the war? They surely must have!"

"Well, for the most part. A nosey woman with Tory connections started a vile rumor that I was involved romantically with Abe Woodhull! What sheer nonsense!"

"People can be so cruel! I had a rumor started about me, but at least it was a nice one! Some

184

people said that Christiansburg, Virginia was named in my honor!"

I laughed heartily, but Nancy didn't.

"Well, with what you did to support the Patriots, it should have been!"

I giggled, and thanked her. "If you ever make it down to the Allegheny Divide, please look me up!" I said.

She smiled and asked if we would like to stay for lunch. I told her that we must be headed home as the weather was threatening. She said that she understood.

Michael had just taken the whole thing in. It was my venture and he was always unselfish.

"Thank you, young man, for your service to our country." She looked into Michael's eyes and smiled.

"You are very welcome madam!" Michael returned the smile and tipped his hat.

It was snowing lightly as we left. We went immediately to the ferry and made our way steadily toward home.

Anna Smith Strong

Chapter Thirty-one

We had a pleasurable journey home with only minor delays because of the weather. We stayed at inns all the way to avoid being out in the harsh cold at night.

Important events were transpiring so quickly in our new country that it almost made my head spin in 1792. These things affected us all! On 20 February, The Postal Service Act establishing a nationwide Post Office Department was signed by President Washington.

On 2 April the Congress Coinage Act established the United States dollar as our official unit of currency! The Mint in Philadelphia started the ongoing task of producing coins based on the dollar. It was patterned after the Spanish "real-coin dollar," also known as a peso, which had long been used by Spanish settlers in New Spain and was readily available in America. The Mint was placed under the auspices of the U.S. Department of Treasury in the capable leadership of Alexander Hamilton. We previously had coins called Continentals, but these had become worth only a small fraction of their face value. I knew that we were on the right track with our monetary system.

On 1 June Kentucky was cut off of Virginia and became the fifteenth state. Three days later, Isaac Shelby was inaugurated as its first governor.

On 13 October the cornerstone was laid in the foundation of the executive mansion in Washington in the parcel of land cut off of Virginia and Maryland named the District of Columbia. The day before had been the 300th anniversary of Columbus' arrival in the New World, and a holiday was established and celebrated in New York City honoring him. Then the Capitol District was named for him, but the town, for our President.

There was plenty going on right here in Virginia, as well.

On 10 November 1792 the General Assembly of Virginia passed an act officially establishing the town of Christiansburgh, spelled with an "h" on the end back then, reportedly named for Colonel William Christian, the Virginia Continental soldier and politician, whom I mentioned earlier, who drew up the Fincastle Resolutions. He also founded Fort Henry in Louisville, Kentucky. I guess it didn't hurt that, like William Campbell, he was a brother-in-law of Governor Patrick Henry.

Then to cap these events off, there was a lot of jubilation when Washington was reelected President on 3 December. He made me proud to be an American.

Colonel William Christian

Chapter Thirty-two

I knew that there were a number of outstanding women who were instrumental in serving the Patriots during the war, and even before. But several of them were wives of our Presidents. Women like Martha Custis Washington, Dolly Madison and Abigail Adams.

There was even Mercy Otis Warren, wife of James Warren, President of the Massachusetts Provincial Congress who was a Paymaster General of the Continental Army during the war. What I wouldn't have given to meet her and hear how as a writer she became the "Conscience of the American Revolution." I have been blessed to read a lot of poems which she wrote that were passed on to me by Agnes. So often my heart was encouraged by her words while Michael was still away at war. But these ladies were all out of my ability to meet. I was even more impressed by bravery and courageous acts.

There was still one more of my women heroes that I hadn't met that I felt I might actually be blessed enough to make her acquaintance. And Nancy Ann Hart didn't live as far away as Anna

Nancy Strong. It was uncanny how similar their names were! Nancy was only down the road a ways in North Georgia. In September of '93 I went to Michael and begged him to accompany me this one last time. I was sixty-three years old and knew that I would likely not feel like traveling that far much longer.

Michael was so kind, laying aside his duties, asking his brothers to take care of them while we were away. This time I used my head, not my forceful determination. Neither snow nor harsh temperatures to contend with in either extreme.

The trip went quickly. Roads were improving all throughout the South. The war had been good in that respect, for the states had made sure that our Continental Army had been able to travel easily about all sections of our new country.

We arrived at Nancy's home in only four days. There were, of course, no servants or fancy tea sets. But there I met one of the bravest women I have ever encountered. As with Anna Strong, I asked her to tell me her story in her own words. I beseeched Michael to help me take notes and he was more than happy to do so. With his notes and mine I am able to tell the story fairly close to the way she gave it that day.

She told me a lot of stories that I had already heard. Things like her friendship with the Cherokees, her Indian name and disguising herself like a crazy man to act as a spy. They were actually true! Now I had heard them straight from the horse's mouth.

Then I asked her to relate to me some of the most important details of the trials and adventures that she went through during the war. What I heard shocked even me.

"One day my children discovered a British soldier spyin' on our home and I doused him with boilin' water that I was usin' to make lye soap before turnin' him over to the Patriot forces. You should've heard him scream!

"Another time, six British soldiers entered our home to question me about assistin' a Patriot in escaping from the reg'lars. I'd really done it, you know. The soldiers then demanded that I feed 'em, and so I agreed to host 'em, putin' out a fair amount of vittles and drink. With a bit o' help from my twelve-year old daughter, Sukey, I managed to remove several of the soldiers' muskets from the stack they had piled up in the corner of the room without them suspectin' anything. I had passed two of their muskets to Sukey through a hole in the wall before them smart soldiers even noticed! I told the soldiers to remain where they were, and when one of 'em got up to come at me, I shot 'im dead and wounded one of the others before takin' the other four men hostage. Sukey ran to let Benjamin know what I done then came back to the cabin. After figurin' on whether to shoot the remainin' men or hang 'em, we and our neighbors decided to just hang them goldern enemy soldiers from a tree in the yard.

I gasped. I didn't know what to say. I considered myself tough, but there was no way I could have done that! Or would have.

Nancy Morgan Hart

Chapter Thirty-three

As my younger sons married and left home, I knew that it was time for me to do something different with my life.

On 2 January '92, young George wed Mary Kirby, daughter of Henry and Mary, dear friends of mine. Henry was Samuel's brother, who had also deeded land to the town.

Then on 8 March, John took Mary's sister, Nancy for his bride. It has not been uncommon in our county for brothers to marry sisters. It also makes their children almost like brothers and sisters themselves. I love to see them together now. Being a grandmother has been such a great blessing to me.

On 5 September in '97 William married Mary Martin... well everyone calls her Polly. She is the daughter of fine parents, Philip and Catherine Martin who live only a few miles away from me.

Michael named one of his daughters after my little angel, Barbara, and later William named one of his for Elizabeth. It kept their names and memories alive, and made me so happy. Well, I will just list them all! My grandchildren have filled a great void in my life. I feel so blessed.

Michael and Cathy have four: Michael II, Nancy, Barbara, Sally and Emmanuel.

William and Polly have five: Nancy, Elizabeth, William II, Martin, Jacob and George.

John and Nancy just have two: another Elizabeth and Hiram.

George the younger and Mary have the largest family of all! James, Christina, Celinda, Delilah, Diana, Henry, John, Jane, Juliet, and finally, George III, just born last year. On 5 December '97, George, Junior was appointed a Constable under Captain James Craig.

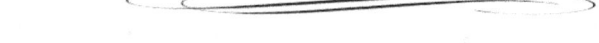

In February of '98, I heard from Agnes that Jacob Snidow had married George's step-daughter, Mary Hanky. It seems in a small town all families eventually intermarry.

That year I let my younger sons divide the rest of my land and continue farming it. The contract with the House of Burgesses, of course, was no longer valid. All I wanted to care for was the house and a few acres around it, including our cemetery, which were just outside the limits of the town of Christiansburgh.

Michael purchased another two tracts totaling 1,001 acres near Elk Creek and was considered one of the more prosperous farmers in Wythe County, where he lived.

In '93 Grayson County was split off of Wythe County and that is where this new land was. Still, like his mother, he refused to own slaves.

I had a lot of experience as a young lady working in and managing a hostel and as a hostess in a tavern. I had long planned on turning my home into a tavern. The right time had come.

I petitioned the county officials for a license and not a one voted against me. There was no other woman in Christiansburg who owned a business without a husband. I knew then that I was revered for the stand I had taken against my Tory husband. They were now adhering to the sophisticated revisions made to date in the laws regulating taverns in the state of Virginia. The Comprehensive Law of 1705 had first been changed in 1748, and then once again in 1779. There were now more specific laws governing the consuming of alcohol on the premises. The county justices had fixed rates regarding fees charged for drinks, food, lodging and even horse feed. Tavern owners were not permitted to extend credit to seamen or servants, so I solved that problem. I allowed no credit whatsoever! All services were cash on the barrelhead.

I felt lucky that John was one of the justices. I knew he was at least partially responsible for my being awarded my license in the first place, and I sure wouldn't do anything to let him down.

Michael helped me make some more changes, like building a bar and stocking the kitchen with whisky, and ale. And we ordered a brown cow— oh, for those who may not know, that's a barrel of beer.

Then with the help of my younger sons they built some extra stalls on the barn to provide a livery for overnight travelers. They made sure there was plenty of shelled corn and fodder to feed the horses of our overnight guests.

Chapter Thirty-four

I opened the tavern on April Fools' Day in '98! In the Netherlands, April Fools' Day is attributed to the Dutch victory in 1572 at Brielle, where the Spanish Duke Alverez de Toledo was defeated. There is even a Dutch proverb about the Duke losing his glasses on April first. I needed something humorous to get people's attention.

Michael hung my sign on the porch: "**Christy's Ordinary - Rest and Entertainment for the Weary Traveler**."

I had purchased several nice round tables, plenty of chairs and bar stools brought in from Lancaster. I put up placards in the dining room of the tavern advocating the rights of women, and due respect for all. At least the men didn't try to go against me. I was determined to advance the cause of women in the Virginia Colony by starting right here in Montgomery County.

It didn't take long for word to spread that there was a feisty little lady running an ordinary just out of Christiansburg on the Great Road. Word of mouth was working well. I got a piano brought in, a young man named Billy to play it and two fancy gals to wear frilly clothes and dance and sing. Through the years these have come and gone. But anything further than normal flirtation was always strictly forbidden at work.

I did not bring in a billiard table due to the Virginia law made against tavern gambling in 1779. There is no way that I would be paying a fine of $150.00 levied for allowing one in my ordinary.

I told everyone that neither I, nor my employees, were permitted to take part in card games in any way. If betting was done, I said, it must be under the table and kept on the low down. I knew that I could not monitor all activity going on. Men will do what they want, but I didn't have to be a part of it.

Another law provided for only minimum alcohol consumption on the Lord's Day. I refused to serve any alcoholic beverages at all on Sunday and caught a lot of flak from customers for it. But I am in control here and run a tight ship. If someone has a drink on the Sabbath they must bring in their own bottle.

I also hired a fine lady in her forties named Minnie to be my cook. She was known all over the area for her fine abilities at preparing meals for special occasions such as weddings and parties. Now she is exclusive with Christy's Ordinary and has been a real drawing card for my establishment.

All guns had to be left outside in their saddlebags or checked with my doorman; a tough fellow I hired named Joe. He had a somber looking mug and burly frame. Everybody knew better than to take any arms inside. Card games were usually peaceful, but I personally stepped in if it appeared that there was any trouble brewing.

I owed so much to my children for sticking by me. But my precious Michael passed away in August of '98, not long after helping me open the tavern. His heart failed, the doctor said. My own heart sank to the lowest depths. After Michael's death I had a hard time coping with life. He had been my solid rock since George's departure. I would just lie in bed in the mornings and not want to face another day. I had neighbors help with the tavern until I could gain some composure.

Thank God, Cathy comforted me the best way she knew how, though I knew her heart was also tearing into a million pieces.

I returned to praying and Bible reading as I had done growing up and started attending church services in the little Presbyterian Church that is now established in town. Most people around here who are Christians are Presbyterians, because the lion's share of 'em are Scotch or Scotch-Irish. I have felt a strong pull to God, and I'm glad.

Chapter Thirty-five

Christy's Ordinary has truly been a joy in my later years. It has served as an inn, a dining hall, a bar and a stage coach stop. It is smaller than James Craig's, and has never reached the glory that his did, but it has been all I could handle, even with the fine help I have obtained.

Being on the Great Road, however, has been a real boon. Especially since the tavern is a stagecoach stop. Even William Clark, the explorer and partner of Meriwether Lewis who led the expedition to the Louisiana Territory back in '04—'06, has stopped here to have a brew or two on more than one occasion on his trips west. In fact, he lived in Christiansburg for some time and married his dear wife, Julia, over in Fincastle. I found him a delightful gentleman with whom to visit.

When my grandchildren—and great grand-children, now—want to come around, I just ask their mothers to bring them in the mornings before the rowdies come in. Sometimes we get jaw-me-downs and occasionally someone would get as drunk as Davy's sow. But I also have a stiff hand to prevent trouble and I hired a brawny local man, called Bob, as a chucker out to back me up. If he is not around, and something is boiling over, I just yell for Joe.

All of my employees have become close friends. I have always treated them the way I would want to be treated were our roles reversed.

Even at my age, on occasion, older men have flirted with me and wanted me to sit with them at their table in the tavern and have a drink. It has always flattered me, but I had no interest in beginning a new relationship in my sixties or beyond. I guess I really was still a bit attractive for an older woman and I have always kept myself clean and well-groomed. But I have made new friends of regular customers, both local ones and those who regularly travel into Tennessee on this road.

We all laugh when someone brings up the name of our town and makes a wisecrack about it being named in my honor. I think some of them still believed the story. For them the statements and questions were sincere.

One day when I was working in the tavern a young couple came by for an evening meal. They were dark complexioned and I asked them where they were from. The gentleman was soft spoken, and he said they had arrived by ship in Norfolk from Portugal a few weeks before and were coming here to look for work. He told me that people in Virginia had mistakenly referred to them as Black Dutch, but they were actually of Moorish descent.

Somehow I felt a connection to them, and told them about my great grandmother and my descent from the true Black Dutch.

The wife, Agueda, had experience as a waitress, so I hired her and told the husband, Balduino, that he could do odd jobs for me for the time being. I put them up in my inn until they could find other, more permanent quarters.

They became dear friends straight away and Agueda is still working for me, waiting tables and helping Minnie in the kitchen. Balduino found work as a sales clerk at a general store on Main Street.

By summer 1800 I was able to buy and sell land. When I would hear of someone wanting to sell, I would saddle up Carrie and go visiting. I was getting copies of *The Star and Herald,* the local paper which had just started publishing that year in Christiansburg and listed land for sale. Strangely, sales of land became another good source of income for me and since my boys had their own places now, I knew they were not in need of property, so I let people know to come by the ordinary and deal with me on price. I have never found it necessary to place a newspaper advertisement because it was well known all about Montgomery County that I was doing this. I always made $100 or two on any piece of land or I would hold it till I could.

The other day I read an article in the local newspaper that took my thoughts back to a wonderful memory, but gave me sadness as well. It stated that the elk have almost all been either killed off by hunters or driven farther west. The closest ones being sighted now are in the western part of Kentucky. The way the trend is going, they won't be there for long. To stay positive I must return my thoughts to more pleasant recent happenings.

An interesting man whom I met here was a young fellow by the name of David Crockett. He lived in Christiansburg for quite some time from 1800 to 1802. I was shopping for a hat in John

Snider's Shop on West Main Street back in the fall of '02 and this handsome young gentleman waited on me. He was dressed rather oddly, as he had on a jacket made from soft leather. He did sell me a stylish hat, though, and nodded his head at me when I left, bidding me g'day.

I asked Agnes if he was any relation to her and she said not that she knew of.

He had talked to me for quite a spell. First, upon arriving in town, he told me that he had worked for a month as a farmhand for James Caldwell for $.50 a day. Then he served as an apprentice at *The Star and Herald*, for a short time. They just couldn't afford to keep him, he said. We never had a newspaper here before, and I sure hope it stays around. It has helped in my real estate dealings, but it isn't yet anything like the big town papers.

Crockett then went to work for Elijah Griffith, a local hatter, for his room and board and a chance to learn the trade, agreeing to work for a four year period. But he had been told that his work there was unsatisfactory to his employer. After eighteen months, he got up one morning to learn that he was out of work. Broke and unemployed, he hired on at John Snider's Hattery Shop, where I met him, which enabled him to earn enough money, I found out later, to return to Tennessee.

I have heard a lot of talk about his great story-telling ability back in Morristown, Tennessee where his father, John Crockett, has a tavern on the stage coach road coming into Virginia, an extension of this road. Folks like to gossip to me about other taverns they have been to. The man who told me about him said he is married to a well-bred lady over there. Folks seem to think young Crockett is going places in life.

Chapter Thirty-six

On 14 August 1805, my dear, dear friend John Montgomery passed away at the medical facility at Fort Chiswell. This time it was me consoling Agnes, who brought him home for burial. It felt like the end of an era for me. For fifty-five years he was a major part of my life and Agnes being my dearest friend, the loss for me was brutal.

I brought her over to spend some time with me in the private quarters in my home on a Sunday afternoon and we talked for hours about all we had been through together. Raising our children and their playing together. Even the loss of my baby girls and my two oldest boys. Neither of us brought up George, though.

Minnie fixed our dinner and we had a fine time, as much as we could under those circumstances. What a spectacular friend.

I am reminded of the verse in the Bible, in Proverbs, chapter 18, verse 24, that says, "A man that hath friends must shew himself friendly;" of course it applies to women too. Agnes and I have always been like that.

A shocking incident happened not far from here, in Downtown Christiansburg, on 9 May 1808 which will never be forgotten. It is known as the Lewis-McHenry Duel. That was quite a story in itself.

I knew Thomas Lewis, a young lawyer who was living with his sister, Catherine, and brother-in-law, Joseph King, a storekeeper, beside the courthouse square. He was General Andrew Lewis' son. I was aware that he and John McHenry were friends, though John was quite a bit older. In a small community everyone pretty much knows everyone else. Thomas came in the tavern one day and told me what they were going to do.

"Why on earth would you agree to something like that, Tom?" I asked him.

"John and I have a political difference that we just can't settle. Tom Bowyer has hounded us both to death over it. He told us that if we didn't agree to a duel we were both cowards!"

"Now, Tom! You know you aren't a coward! Don't let Bowyer bully you like that! What has he got to do with this, anyway?"

"Well, it's a bit late. I was mighty angry with both of them and told him I would go through with it. I think I'm faster than John, anyway!"

"You didn't tell me what Tom Bowyer has to do with this!" I said.

"I thought a lot about that. I think he wants me to win. I think he wants a piece of land that John owns and wants him out of the way!"

I felt totally helpless. Who was I to think I could make a bull-headed man change his mind when his honor was at stake?

No women were invited, or I think I may have gone myself. That morning, five men, Tom, John and their seconds, along with an attending surgeon, Doctor John Floyd, gathered in a small grove of saplings. Bowyer was Tom's second, James Charlton was John's.

Tom, with a solemn look, the newspaper said, went to kiss his sister's baby goodbye, just in case he didn't make it.

Both men, I was told, were dressed in new suits with rows of brass buttons. Thomas had been the challenger, so John chose the weapons and stance. Rifles at thirty paces. Surely Thomas had been sorry at that point, because in other duels this had led to an almost certain death for both men, and both were skilled marksmen.

Bowyer and Charlton stepped off the distance of thirty paces. Lewis was placed at a hickory sapling; McHenry beside another sapling. The article I read didn't say what kind.

The seconds walked to the center of the field to examine and prepare the weapons. Charlton spoke out loudly: "Bowyer, we have tried these men in every way and found them to be truly brave, let us load their rifles without the fatal lead bullets."

Bowyer snapped back, "We didn't come here for child's play, this is man's work!"

Charlton's effort having failed, the seconds loaded the rifles and took them to the principals.

The article said that then the signal was given by Bowyer, "One, two, three, fire!"

McHenry, though twenty years the elder, apparently fired a split second before Lewis, but

Lewis, though shot through the heart, fired as he fell, and both men were mortally wounded.

Lewis died instantly, but McHenry fell slowly, going down as if he had some control over his fall!

Charlton rushed to McHenry, who motioned him away. "Go see how it is with poor Tom," he said.

Charlton and the good doctor returned to McHenry and informed him that Lewis was dead.

It was as though he regretted his actions. "Poor Tom, poor Tom!" he said, "He was the best friend I ever had!"

"The little fellow pinked me badly," said the doctor. "He was shot through the liver."

If only Tom had listened to me! He would likely have lived many years and helped a lot of people.

Thomas was taken to Shawsville for burial, so I wasn't able to attend his service, but I paid his precious sister a visit the next time I was in town. I asked her how old Tom was, as I had thought it impolite to ask him. She said he was only 22.

Then, a few months later, I left Emma in charge at my ordinary and rode up to Madison Cemetery to pay my respects. I thought I owed him that. The grave is unmarked, but I was able to locate it with the help of a local lady.

That senseless rifle duel led to the passage of the Barbour Bill on 10 June 1810, named for speaker of the Virginia House of Delegates, James Barbour, outlawing dueling in Virginia.

Doctor Floyd turned politician and was elected to the Virginia House of Delegates in 1814; then went on to the U.S. House of Representatives where he now serves. I met him when he was running for the Virginia House and was quite impressed with him. I think he would make a fine governor some day.

It seems that what Job said in the Bible has also been applied in my life more than a person should have to go through. "Man is few of days and full of trouble."

Well, at least I have been blessed with days. Maybe it is because I honored my father and mother, like the Bible says. But my life has certainly had its share of trouble.

I mentioned earlier that our sons were all short in stature. Michael Junior married a fine girl, of average height. However, their little ones are dwarfs. Their names are Hiram and Roxana. Their size just makes me love them more and wish that I could be able to care for them myself; but, alas, that is impossible. I just make it a special point to show them in every way how very special they are.

I hope they make the most of their lives and show others that they are proud to be so special.

Chapter Thirty-seven

Then my poor heart broke apart once more! In April 1812 my best friend and shoulder to cry on, Agnes, passed away at Fort Chiswell, just like her husband. As always, it was the only place we could get medical attention anywhere around and John had served there and gotten to know the doctors well. We now had a better road leading to Ingles Ferry to get there, and it had shortened the trip to around 38 miles.

Again, I was at a very low ebb in life, but the loss of so many in my own family had made me a tough old bird. I decided I wasn't going to live the rest of my life in mourning. After her funeral I spent some time with the Montgomery children, now all grown, and their children, along with my own children and grandchildren, in a celebration of the lives of John and Agnes. They were all very grateful for my friendship and promised to stay in touch, which some of them have done. I love them like my own children.

George's stepdaughters both married and his new wife passed away. None of them ever came around me, of course. George was totally homeless before he died. Jacob Snidow, husband of his stepdaughter, Mary, had taken over as the overseer for the poor in Montgomery County, the position previously held by his ex-father-in-law, Thomas Burke. Jacob was paid $30.00 to keep him the final year of his life, which ended in 1813.

We have now come through another violent conflict with Britain which had no sense happening. It was known as the War of 1812, although it lasted into 1815. The war was all due to the simple fact that Britain was jealous over America's independence and the Royal Navy refused to stop seizing our citizens in ships on the open seas and forcing them into the service of the Crown. This had happened to over 15,000 Americans who had been so seized between 1793 and 1812 before our government declared war. I believe anyone would say "Enough is enough!" And that was far more than enough!

Britain was also supplying arms to Algonquian peoples, the northern tribes, who had fought with them in the French and Indian War. These tribes were coming into our country raiding and hindering our expanse to the western frontier. Naturally our ire was up.

Why, even right here in Christiansburg, companies of militia were organized at the very beginning of the war! Thank God it was all on a volunteer basis and none of my family members were involved. On a local note, Captain William Pepper's Rifle Company became a part of the Virginia Volunteer Regiment.

Captain Pepper took his troops and left Christiansburg on 13 September 1813. They marched through Petersburg, I read, on their way to Norfolk where they were stationed.

After finishing that term of service in March of '14, being discharged and returning home a second requisition of troops was made upon Montgomery County! With Captain James Hoge in command, it headed to Norfolk to serve its term.

The British fleet under Admiral George Cockburn devastated a lot of villages and farms along the coast, burning bridges and destroying houses, and robbing people of their crops, stock and slaves. I only hope those poor slaves were given their freedom. They even plundered churches of their communion services and murdered sick folks right in their beds! What a horrible travesty!

Then General Ross marched to Washington and in August burned the new Capitol Building, Congressional Library, other public buildings and records, and private homes and store-houses!

Thank God for First Lady Dolly Madison, a true woman hero! With great presence of mind she enlisted the help of her servants and saved many of the treasures of the country! One of the greatest of these was the Lansdowne portrait painted by Gilbert Stuart, which had been a gift from former British Prime Minister, William Petty, 1st Marquess of Lansdowne. It is a magnificent full-length, life-size canvas painting of George Washington and was taken from the frame by her fifteen-year-old servant boy, Paul Jennings, I read. If only I could have only been there I would have also gladly helped that dear soul!

Ross then marched on Baltimore on 12 September and this is where he was mortally shot by two patriot mechanics! Both of the mechanics were then instantly killed by British soldiers, but they had done their part and will long be remembered!

The Lansdowne Portrait

It was during the bombardment of Fort McHenry over the next two days that Francis Scott Key, a Maryland lawyer who was in prisoner release negotiations on board a British vessel, wrote the poem, "The Defence of Fort McHenry," which became the patriotic song, The Star Spangled Banner. It was soon set to the music of a British tune composed by John Stafford Smith for a men's social club in London back in the 1770s.

Unbelievably to me, there was some Federalist opposition in the U.S. to going to war. Especially in New England. They blamed President Madison, calling it his war! Horse pucky!

Though Britain had a change of Prime Ministers, it was too late for them to avoid continuing the conflict on new fronts. It was back to our trying to invade Canada.

Peace negotiations began in August 1814 and the Treaty of Ghent was signed on 24 December. This treaty was not unanimously ratified in the Senate until 17 February, which I kept as my 85th birthday, in '15.

Word came to me in March that Mary Ingles had passed away. That was another great loss for all who met and loved her.

It is now 1818 and I feel that I have little time left in this world, but am ready to go. I have learned to live one day at a time and trust in the Creator to give me peace of mind.

I hope that whoever may read my story will find it interesting and informative.

I am thankful for the prosperity with which I have been blessed, but I know that I'm just a poor wayfaring stranger traveling through this world of woe. I think I was inspired by Mercy Warren. I have written a poem about that which I have passed on to Michael's son, Emmanuel, who has a keen ear for music. I have asked him to put a melody to it. He has taken up the banjo and loves folk music. He travels about to folk music shows and knows a lot of people.

I pray that my family will fare well in this new and glorious land and that God will long bless America.

Epilogue

Christiana Crewey died on 27 July 1818 at the age of 88. She was laid to rest on her property near the corner of what is now North Franklin and Depot Streets in Christiansburg.

Historian James Robert "Bob" Shelton wrote a remarkable tribute to her titled "The Legend of Christiana Crewey" published in Mary E. Lindon's *Virginia's Montgomery County* (Montgomery Museum and Lewis Miller Regional Art Center, 2009, pages 569-572).

The story about the town being named for her never completely died, largely because of a manuscript written by H. L. Price, *Outlines of Montgomery County Families, Volume II*, penned in the mid 1800s. It is in the Price Family Collection, 1840-1905, held in the Special Collections Room at Virginia Tech in Blacksburg. Price states of Christiana Crewey, "...she gave the Courthouse Square to the town of Christiansburg, which was named for her."

The Price family from Germany settled in that area in the 1740s.

For whom the town was actually named is clouded by history and never really proven. Some of Christiana's descendants, according to Bob Shelton, are staunch believers to this day that the town was indeed named for her. The story was passed down by family members. More than one website still makes this claim.

Other modern historic accounts indicate that the courthouse was built on the land donated by James Craig and the town was named in honor of Colonel William Christian.

Apparently the name George was not as resented by his descendants, as it has lived on in his offspring for the generations to come, even to the present day.

According to Bob Shelton, the family stated that the original land grant was for 3,500 acres, and was reportedly in the hands of Robert Craig and his wife, Virginia Roberts Walters as late as the early 1900s. According to Shelton, it is said that Eula Walters Brooks borrowed the document and never returned it. Her sister, Ella Walters Stevens said that Eula had it framed and hanging on her living room wall for many years. Eula moved into the Methodist Retirement Home in Brandenton, Florida, where she died in 1974.

No record has ever been found substantiating such a large grant was ever made to George

Some assumed that the grant was made for service in the French and Indian War, but this does not hold water. George was not educated and did not serve as an officer, if he did serve in that war. Only officers received large grants. Captains were only granted 3,000 acres.

Four of Michael Junior's children turned out to be dwarfs; the others, Catharine and William, having been born after Christiana's death.

A slave owner, William Macon Waller, walking a coffle of about two dozen slaves along the overland route from Amherst County Virginia to Mississippi through Wythe County in the fall of 1847, met the family and was fascinated with them. Writing letters to his wife, Sarah, about his adventures, in one he related a fascinating story about this family.

Newspaper articles from across the Eastern U.S. state that the family preformed as "The Virginia Dwarf Family" with Hiram, the oldest, using the stage name "Major Walters." These included the

Charlotte Observer (North Carolina), the *Augusta Constitutionalist* (South Carolina), the *Richmond Dispatch* (Virginia) and the *Detroit Free Press* (Michigan). It is likely from some of these accounts that they traveled for some time with the Barnum and Bailey Circus. The Detroit paper printed an article about their appearance at Barnum's American Museum in New York.

Roxana, Hiram and Catharine on stage

There are stories which report Hiram, Roxana and Catharine performing in Europe. One account says that they were even presented to Queen Victoria. No proof of this seems to exist.

**Barnum's American Museum,
Broadway, New York City**

Nevertheless, after June of 1861 the group was never heard from again, and there are various tales about the demise of most of them. Some said they died of smallpox in New York, others say London. It is certain that showman John Burnell married their sister, Nancy, and is buried in New York.

William, however, was quite a colorful character after he left the group and the entertainment world. He married, and in April of 1859 was running a grocery store in upper East Tennessee, in a small town named Union.

A man named Elijah Cross came into the store and reportedly started making improper advances to his unusually attractive wife. He ordered Cross to leave and he refused. William ran into another room and got a gun, blocking the door to prevent Cross' escape. When he attempted to leave through a window, Walters shot and killed him.

The following incomplete account appeared in the *Richmond Daily Dispatch* on April 23, 1859:

FATAL AFFRAY.—On Thursday of last week, a man named Elijah Cross, living at Union, Tenn., was shot by William Walters, and died in a few hours. Walters is a dwarf, a native of Wythe county, Va. He had recently gone to Union, where he had opened a grocery. Cross was a dissipated man, and while at the grocery got into an altercation with Walters, who ordered him from the premises. Refusing to leave, Walters ran to an adjoining room for a gun, when Cross attempted to make his escape from the house by the window, but was shot before he could effect his exit.

According to an article in the *North Carolinian*, published at the time in Elizabeth City, William was charged with first degree murder and convicted.

It is uncertain what happened after that. An article in the North Carolina newspaper, *New Bern Daily Progress*, William was granted a new trial and the case was moved to Greeneville, Tennessee. Some say it was overturned according to the Appetite 4 History website.

Regardless, that is not important, because, on December 30, 1863, William's hometown paper, *The Wytheville Dispatch*, carried the large headline, "Murder in Wythe County."

Two different stories were told about what happened. It is known that William, who was said to be 3 feet 2 inches tall, was killed by a man named Roberts. *The Dispatch* reported that Walters was attempting to purchase a still from Roberts and got into a heated argument. This article did not explain the method of the killing. The Wytheville paper did report that the killer was still on the loose.

A rival between newspapers apparently got reporters digging deeper—or possibly fabricating. A later report by *The Bristol News*, Bristol, Tennessee, states the following:

"The *Wytheville Enterprise* says the dwarf Wm. Walters was not killed in the manner stated by the correspondent of the *Currier Journal*, but that his taking off occurred in a gambling spree near Cullop's mill in Wythe Co., Va., with one Steve Roberts a wooden legged individual, who, because Walters won all his money, cut his throat from ear to ear, and then limped out of Virginia into Kentucky, and has never been heard from since.

"Well, well! Cock Robin being dead, it is immaterial who killed him."

After the death of James Craig a new brick plantation house was built at Hans Meadow which is still there today.

George Washington called Hans Meadows "a mustering place for frontiersmen to take action against threatening Indians."

New Hans Meadow Plantation House
built in 1849

A lot happened in this area during the War Between the States which is recorded in my previous novel, *Turning Point at Gettysburg*.

After the Civil War, Charles S. Schaeffer founded Hill School in 1866 to educate former slaves. It later became Christiansburg Industrial Institute.

Beginning in 1896, Booker T. Washington served as an adviser for the Institute and visited Christiansburg several times.

Many of the descendants of George and Christiana still live in and around Montgomery County Virginia.

My great grandfather, John Meddow "Med" St. Clair married Sally Bell Walters, George and Christiana's great granddaughter, a descendant of their son George A., who was to become my great-great grandmother.

My father, Marvin W. St. Clair, was born and brought up in Christiansburg, not far from the Walters farm, and often spoke of his Walters cousins.

I lived there for about two and a half years as a toddler on my grandmother, Lula Graham St. Clair's farm on Falling Branch.

The Walters Cemetery that I was able to locate, was grown up and in much need of repair. It is out Highway 615 near Riner, seeming to indicate that the original Walters homestead, hence Christiana's tavern, was south of town. However, all dated markers are from burials in the 1800s.

There are four indentations indicating graves with no markers. George A. Walters' faded headstone shows his date of birth as June 14, 1767 and date of death as November 3, 1863. He was ninety-six years and four months old. His wife Mary's stone stands nearby. Her dates are March 8, 1771 to July 17, 1845.

Walters Farm Cemetery

The story of Mary Draper Ingles has been one of the most endearing and oft told ones in Virginia history. The trail which she followed on her journey home bears her name.

A bronze statue of her is included in the Virginia Women's Monument on the grounds of the State Capitol in Richmond.

Radford University, located near Draper's Meadows, has halls named Draper Hall and Ingles Hall in honor of her.

A statue of Mary stands in front of the Boone County Public Library, and an identical one was erected at Radford Cultural Heritage Park near the Glencoe Museum in October 2016.

Another monument, built from the chimney of her home where she returned in 1755, is dedicated to her and is located in West End Cemetery in Radford.

An elementary school in Tad, West Virginia bears her name.

Kentucky Route 8 in Campbell, Braken and Mason counties is officially named Mary Ingles Highway.

Ingles Ferry is listed on the National Register of Historic Places.

The Virginia Tech Library in Blacksburg holds documents once owned by her.

Mary Ingles Cultural Heritage Park adjacent to Radford Visitors Center includes a brass cast from the statue at Boone County Public Library.

The Mary Ingles Chapter of the National Society Daughters of the American Revolution is located at Fort Thomas, Kentucky.

A novel titled *Follow the River* by James Alexander Thom published by Ballantine Books in 1986 became a national best seller.

In 1995, a TV movie, *Follow the River*, starring Sheryl Lee and Ellen Burstyn was made about the capture and escape of Mary Ingles based on Thom's book.

A historic novella was written about the Mary Draper Ingles story by Mary R. Furbee titled *Shawnee Captive; The Story of Mary Ingles*, published in 2001 by Quarter Press in Charleston, West Virginia.

A short 58 minute film about Mary Draper Ingles for show in museums, camps and parks titled *The Captives* starring Elliot Miller and Sarah "Sadie" Jones was released in 2004.

In 2007 American Movie Classics aired a Revolutionary War period drama titled *TURN: Washington's Spies* in which the story of Anna Strong was featured. She was played by Heather Lind. It is available on DVD as Anna Strong: A Spy During the American Revolution.

Both Daniel Boone and David "Davy" Crockett went on to be popularized in American folklore.

Unfortunately, their legends are both, at times more fiction than fact.

David Crockett, made famous during his lifetime, has a state park named for him in Tennessee, and had numerous movies and films made honoring his bravery. It turns out that he most likely was one of the five to seven "Texans" who surrendered to General Castrillon on March 6, 1836, and were executed.

The women featured in this book were never captured and all showed outstanding bravery.

On April 4th, 2020, the first ever cup of coffee, accompanied by a pastry, was delivered by drone in Christiansburg. Brugh Coffee, a four-year old roasting and retail company, at the time, partnering with Wing Aviation drone service get the credit.

An historic marker in downtown Christiansburg commemorates the infamous Lewis-McHenry duel.

Dr. John Floyd served in the U.S. House of Representatives from two districts; then was elected Governor of Virginia, serving from March 4, 1830 to March 31, 1834.

From the Alleghany-Elliston-Ironto-Shawsville, LINC Letter, 2018, page 1:

"Thanks to Danny Sisson for letting us know about the unmarked grave of Thomas Lewis of the Lewis–McHenry Duel. Danny takes care of the Madison Cemetery, where Lewis, a grandson of General Lewis, was laid to rest. The Meadowbrook Museum was able to raise funds to purchase a grave marker, and Danny installed it for us. A ceremony celebrating Lewis and our purchase of the marker will be held in the near future."

Thomas Lewis Grave Marker

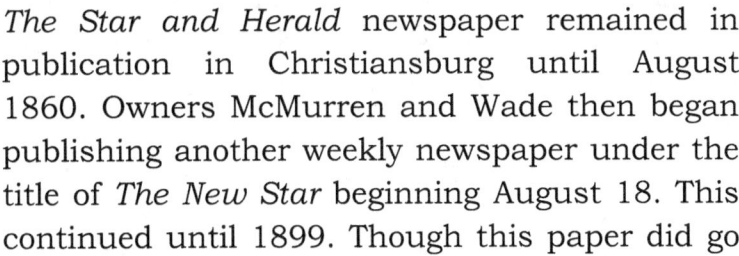

The Star and Herald newspaper remained in publication in Christiansburg until August 1860. Owners McMurren and Wade then began publishing another weekly newspaper under the title of *The New Star* beginning August 18. This continued until 1899. Though this paper did go under, there has always been a newspaper in publication there since the days of Christiana Crewey.

John Sower partnered with William M. Barnitz to make an attempt at another newspaper called *The Weekly Herald* in 1854, but it was short lived.

On December 1, 1869, a new newspaper named the *Montgomery Messenger* was started by John Sower, this time with C.H. Carper, which changed hands on March 24, 1931, but has continued under various names and ownership ever since.

The Montgomery News was also published between 1924 and 1931 by J.A. Osborne, at which time the *Montgomery News* and *Messenger*, created and published by Russell H. Jones replaced both papers until 1967.

On July 11, 1967, W. Brockenbrough took over publication of the *Messenger*, changing its name to *The News Messenger* which served both Christiansburg and Blacksburg until April 30, 1974. At that time the name was changed to *The Blacksburg-Christiansburg News Messenger* until 1978, when it became simply *The News Messenger* until 1993, when it changed ownership. It is still being published today under the title of the *Christiansburg News Messenger.*

Radford was hosting a separate newspaper for a number of years titled *The News Journal,* which halted publication in 1993.

Though authorship of *The Wayfaring Stranger* was never determined, during and for several years after the American Civil War, the lyrics were known as the *Libby Prison Hymn.* This was because the words had been inscribed by a dying Union soldier incarcerated in Libby Prison, a warehouse converted to a notorious Confederate prison in Richmond, Virginia known for its adverse conditions and high death rate. It had been believed that the dying soldier had authored the song to comfort a disabled soldier, but this was not the case since it had been published three years before the Civil War started—in 1858, before Libby Prison was put into service (1862).

Christiansburg has grown from a population of 523 in 1850, to an estimated 22,473 in 2019, with 2020 census figures still not available.

A small community in Montgomery County formed around 1830 is named Lafayette for the

French leader who so ably assisted our country in winning our independence. My uncle, John A. St. Clair lived there many years before his death.

I have visited a number of places from the Colonial and Revolutionary era. Among them are Jamestown, Colonial Williamsburg, Breed's Hill—the hill where the battle of Bunker Hill was fought near Boston—and the Old North Church.

I greatly enjoyed touring George Washington's Estate, Mount Vernon, Virginia and Thomas Jefferson's Monticello at Charlottesville.

I toured our glorious Capitol of Washington, DC and visited the White House and the obelisk monument erected to honor the Father of our Country.

I also stood on the steps of the Federal Building in New York City where Washington was first sworn in as President, and read the sign on the front of the building near his statue commemorating the establishment of the state of Ohio by General Arthur St. Clair.

I have even done research in the Roanoke, Virginia Public Library, and visited Christiansburg on more than one occasion as an adult. My latest visit was July 12 to 14, 2021, in which I visited the Christiansburg Library and the Montgomery Museum. I want to express my deepest appreciation to Curator Sherry Joines Wyatt and her helpful staff.

The Alleghenies and Blue Ridge Mountains offer some of the most scenic and restful spots to visit in the U.S., and there is no shortage of history to be found there. The rebuilt Hans Meadow Plantation House now operates as The Inn at Hans Meadow, a charming bed and breakfast at 1800 Depot Street N.E. Montgomery Museum of Art and History is located at 300 Pepper St. SE, which holds a Heritage Day each August.

Author at Montgomery Museum

About the Author

Stanley J. "Stan" St. Clair is the co-founder of St. Clair Research, found on the Internet at http://www.stclairresearch.com with his distant cousin, Ad Exec Steve St. Clair, who owns and manages the project.

He served as a State Commissioner of the Scottish Clan Sinclair, U.S.A.; first for Georgia, then Tennessee, for several years and as its Eastern Vice President for two years. He was a regular contributor to their official publication **Yours Aye** for a number of years.

He is also a long time member of Kiwanis International, and has served in every position in his local club including several terms as president, and one year as District Lieutenant Governor.

He is a newspaper columnist for **The Southern Standard** and **The Smithville Review**, and the author of more than 20 other published books including the critically acclaimed series **Most Comprehensive Origins of Clichés, Proverbs and Figurative Expressions.**

He is also the sole owner of St. Clair Publications at http://stclairpublications.com. His articles and nostalgic poems have been published in numerous newspapers, magazines and books in the U.S., Canada and the U.K., and on several websites.

He was knighted in 2003 and is an active Knight Lieutenant in the OSMTJ - Knights Templar of America and writes a weekly column for their official online publication, *The Templar Banner*.

He studied creative writing at Tennessee State University and holds a BRE degree from Covington Theological Seminary. He was awarded an honorary PhD in 2020.

Stan was selected for inclusion in the 2022 *Marquis' Who's Who in America*.

Stan and his wife, Rhonda, live in Tennessee.

Reference Sources

Time and Work in Eighteenth Century London,
Hans-Joachim Voth, *The Journal of Economics
History Vol. 58,* No. 1 (Mar, 1998, p 29)
Cambridge University Press, Cambridge, U.K.

*BBC – Travel – Adventures & Experience: The
Tiny 'Country' Between England and Scotland*
https://www.bbc/com/travel/article/20200504
-the-tiny-country-between-england-and-scotland

*Christiansburg, Montgomery County, Virginia, in
the Heart of the Alleghenies* - Lula Porterfield
Givens, pp 1, 5, 9, 10, 18, 19, 39, 40, 41, 42,
43, 49, 50, 51, 59, 60; Edmonds Printing,
Pulaski, Virginia, 1981

Early Adventures on the Western Waters,
Volumes 1, 2 and 3, various pages, Mary B.
Kegley, F.B. Kegley; Green Publishers, U.S.A.,
1980

Virginia in the American Revolution, an exhibition
by the Society of Cincinnati, p 10; Anderson
House, Washington, DC, September 19, 2009 –
March 10, 2010

From Here to Yender: Early Trails and Highway Life, Marion Nicholl Rawson, pp 39, 40; E.P. Dutton & Co., New York, NY, U.S.A., 1932

Tax List of Montgomery County, Virginia, 1782

Record of Certificates of Commissioners of Washington and Montgomery Counties, 1767-1788, Commissioners Certificates, p 159

Black Africans in Seventeenth Century Amsterdam, Dienke Hondious, Renesance and Reformation, Totonto, ON, Canada, 2008

Slavery and Abolition: A journal of Slave and Post-Slave Studies, Volume 32, 2011 –Issue 3: Free Soil –*Access to the Netherlands of Enslaved and Free Black Africans: Exploring Legal and Social Historical Practices in the Sixteenth – Nineteenth Centuries,* Dienke Hondius https://www.tandfonline.com/doi/abs/10.1080/0144039X.2011.588476

The Price Family Collection, 1840-1905, Price, H. L., Outlines of Montgomery County Families, Vol. 2, MS.2012.047, Special Collections, Virginia Tech, Blacksburg, VA.

Survey Book D, Montgomery Co,, VA, 1785, p 242 -April 15, 1785

Survey Book One, Wythe Co., VA 1791-1800, p 159

The 1782 Montgomery County, Virginia Land Tax List - Walters, Michael

Montgomery Co. Virginia Deed Book A, James Douthat, 1787

Grayson County, Virginia - Land Plat Book 1 1793-1794; 1793

The White Loyalists of Williamsburg, Kevin P. Kelly: The Colonial Williamsburg Foundation, Williamsburg, Virginia, 1998

Colonial Williamsburg: Planting with Hope, Ed Schultz https://www.colonialwilliamsburg.org/learn/living-history/planting-hope/

The Friends of the Wild Flower Garden, Inc. Plants of the Eloise Butler Wildflower Garden The oldest public wildflower garden in the United States, Virginia Creeper https://www.friendsofthewildflowergarden.org/pages/plants/virginiacreeper.html

Montgomery Co. Virginia Deed Book A – p 421

Christiansburg Downtown Historic District, p 24, U.S. Department of the Interior, National Park

Service, Washington, DC, 2003

Virginia Soldiers in the Revolution, the Virginia Magazine of History and Biography, pp 57-67; Virginia Historical Society, Richmond, Virginia, January, 1914

1787 Montgomery Co., Va. Delinquent Tax List, Virginia Genealogical Society Quarterly, Vol. XXIV #2, 1 May 1996

The Place To Be: Christiansburg christiansburg.org

Poor Richard's Almanack en.m.wikapedia.org/wiki/Poor_Richard's_ Almanack

Southern Standard, "Army birthday reflections," Thomas B. Vaughn, Col., US Army, Retired, McMinnville, Tennessee, Sun. June 13, 2021

Genealogy.com Genealogy Report, Descendants of George Walters, Herbert W. Doyle

Wythe County, Virginia Will Books 1-2, 1790-1822, James L. Douthat, 1815 - Nov. 14, p 143

The Epidemic of 1759, Smallpox, Winchester, Virginia; Winchester Tales, Facebook

Virginia Genealogical Trails, Land Bound Certificates for Service in the French and Indian Wars. Virginia Colonial Militia 1651-1776; Edited by William Armstrong Crozier, F.R.S. Virginia Record Publications, Vol. 2; The Genealogical Association, New York, NY, 1905

First Continental Congress - ushistory.org

Constitutional Convention (United States) en.m.wikipedia.org

George Washington - en.m.wikipedia.org

The Early American Postal System – https://www.constitutionalfacts.com/founders-library/early-american-postal-system/

Montgomery Museum – https://w2ww.montgomerymuseum.org

Christiansburg, Virginia - https://en.m.wikipedia.org

The Odyssey, Biographies and Memoirs—David Crockett: The Lion of the West - https://www.erenow.net/blog

Benedict Arnold – https://en.m.wikipedia.org

Virginia Line - https://en.m.wikipedia.org

This Day in History, June 18, 1778; British abandon Philadelphia –
https:// www.history.com

History of King George II –
https://www.englishmonarchs.co.uk

John Montgomery, Sr.
https://www.wikitree.com/wiki/Montgomery-836

John Crockett - https://en.m.wikipedia.org

The Culper Spy Ring by History.Com Editors,
March 19, 2010, Updated June 10, 2019
https://www.google.com/amp/topics/American-revolution/culper-spy-ring

Colonial Williamsburg Digital Library: Wheeled Carriages in Eighteenth Century Colonial Virginia. Mary R.M. Goodwin –
https://www.research.colonialwilliamsburg.org/ DigitalLibrary

The South in American Literature: 1607-1800, Jay Hubbell, p 306. Duke University Press, Durham, N.C., 1854

Black Dutch (genealogy)
https://en.wikipedia.org/wiki/Black_Dutch_(ge nealogy)

Battle of Yorktown by History.com Editors
https://www.google.com/amp/s/www.history.
com/amp/topics/american-revolution/seige-of-
yorktown

The Virginia Magazine of History and Biography,
July 1979: Tavern Regulation in Virginia,
Rationale and Reality, Paton Yoder

*"Dun na nGal/Donegal". Placenames Database
of Ireland (logainm.ie), Government of Ireland –
Department of Arts, Heritage and the Gaslacht
and Dublin City University.*

Daily Coffee News by Roast Magazine; The Sky
is The Limit for Brugh Coffee's Delivery by
Drone in Virginia; Howard Bryman, Portland
OR, April 13, 2020

The Roanoke Times: Wing expands drone
delivery options, two Christiansburg businesses
now on board, Roanoke, VA, April 3, 2020

NBC Nightly News, New York, NY May 4, 2021

The Crewey/Cruey Family
https://www.angelfire.com/va2/crewey/

Virginia's Soldiers in the Revolution, Section V,
(*The Virginia Magazine of History and Biography*
Vol. 22, No. 1 (Jan., 1914), pp 57-67

Historic Roads of Virginia, 1777 – 1806, pp ix, 1, 2; Betty E. Spillman and Shirley P. Thomas, New River Historical Society, and Ann Brush Branch, Senior Research Scientist, Virginia Transportation Research Council, Charlottesville, VA, 2008

History of Ingles Ferry - 1937. Fitzpatrick, Francis Burke. Washington, District of Columbia: Library of Congress Photo Duplication Service, 1990. Notes: Microfilm of original typescript (1937, carbon or mimeograph, 65 leaves). Contains history of Ingles Ferry and settlement and biographical sketches of Colonel William Ingles and Mary Draper Ingles.

The Rockingham Connection and the Second Funding of the Whig Party, 1768-1773, pp 119,120, Elofson, W.M., McGill-Queen's University Press, London, U.K., 1996

"The Nigh and Best Way": The Early Development of Roads in Montgomery County, Jim Page and Sherry Joines Wyatt, Montgomery Museum & Lewis Miller Regional Art Center, pp 68 and 76; Christiansburg, VA, 2017

William Clark
https://en.wikipedia.org/wiki/William_Clark
How Settlers Cleared Their Land, Gwen Tuinman
https://gwentuinman.com/2018/05/26/how-settlers-cleared-their-land/

Legends of America, The French and Indian War
https://www.legendsofamerica.com/ah-frenchindianwar/

Gender Roles in Colonial America, Holly Hartman,
pp 1, 2, 4;
https://wou.edu/history/files/2015/08/Holly-Hartman-HST-499.pdf

International Museum of the Horse: Colonial Horses - http://imh.org/exhibits/online

*1765 to 1769 Pennsylvania Maps 1768.*1 Mason and Dixon's Survey
https://www.mapsofpa.com/antiquemsps26b.htm

Mason Dixon Line - https://en.wikipedia.org

Weddings in Colonial Philadelphia
https://www.graemepark.org/weddings

Clara Frances Frazier (Graham)
https://geni.com/people/Clara-Francis-Frazier

Capt. Thomas Burke; geni.com/people/Capt.-Thomas-Burke

William Burke -
https://geni.com/people/William-Burke

George Washington's Culper Spies: Separating Fact from Fiction, Bill Bleyer; https://www.allthingsliberty.com

What Really Happened at Drapers Meadows? The Evolution of a Frontier Legend, Ellen A. Brown, Virginia History Exchange, 2012

The Narrative of Col. John Ingles Relating to Mary Ingles and the Escape from Big Bone Lick, 1824

Trans-Allegheny Pioneers: historical sketches of the first white settlements west of the Alleghenies, John P. Hale, The Graphic Press, Cincinnati, Ohio, 1896

Early Documents Relating to Mary Ingles Escape from Big Bone Lick, James Duvall, M.A., Boone County Public Library, Burlington, KY, 2008

New York Mercury, Mon 26 Jan 1756, p. 3 col. 1; Mon 16 Feb 1756, p 2, cols. 2-3.

Mary Draper Ingles' Return to Virginia's New River Valley, Joan Vannorsdall Schoeder, https://www.blueridgecountry.com

Mary Draper Ingles, well referenced article, https://www.en.wikipedia.org

Col. William Ingles, https://www.geni.com/Col-William-Ingles

Capture and Rescue of the Ingles Family and Killing of Captain Thomas Maxwell, Emory L. Hamilton, sites.roortswen.com/~vavarussel/Indian/46.html

Anna Strong: Women in American Cryptology, https://www.nsa.gov/About-Us/Current-Leadership/Article-View/Article/1620960/anna-strong/

Anna Strong (spy) https://military.wikia.org/wiki/Anna_Strong_ (spy) (Well referenced file)

TCA AMC Picks Up 'Halt & Catch Fire' & 'Turn' to Series, Nellie Andreeva; Deadline.com

American Battlefield Trust: Nancy Hart, https://www.battlefields.org/learn/biographies/nancy-hart

The History of Elk in Virginia https://dwr.virginia.gov/wildlife/elk/history/

Elk Sounds of the Season, August 16, 2020 https://www.montanadecoy.com/news/elk-sounds-of-the-season

Siege of Boston, History.com Editors, Nov. 9, 2009; Feb. 4, 2020, https://www.history.com/topics/american-revolution/eiege-of-boston

Ethan Allen,
https://www.biography.com/.amp/aspolitical-figure/ethan-allen ; Jan. 13, 2016; Jan. 16, 2020

Capture of Fort Ticonderoga, History.com Editors
https://history.com/amp/topics/american-revolution/capture-of-fort-ticonderoga ; Mar. 8, 2010, May 20, 2020

The Story of the Virginia Dwarf Family
https://appetite4history.com/2016/10/05/the-story-of-the-virginia-dwarf-family/

New River Notes: William Patterson Letter 18 July 1779 https://ww.newrivernotes.com

Founders Online: Letter from Thomas Jefferson to William Preston, 7 August 1779
https://www.founders.archives.org

Revolutionary War Times and the Ride of Captain Martin Gambill,
http://rootsweb.ancestry.com/tmetravlr.html

A Visit to the Craig Cemetery in Christiansburg, Jim Glanville; *News Messenger,* Christiansburg, Virginia, p 4, Sat. July 17, 2017

Christiana Crewey,
https://www.werelate.org/wiki/Person:Christia
na_Crewey_(1)

*Summer 1814: Dolley Madison saves
Washington's portrait, with some help,* National
Park Service,
https://www.nps.gov/articles/dolley-madison-
washingtons-
portrait.htm#:~:text=First%20Lady%20Dolley%2
0Madison%20is,attacked%20the%20Capitol%20
in%201814.

*Lansdowne Portrait, Smithsonian's National
Portrait Gallery*
https://en.wikipedia.org/wiki/Lansdowne_portr
ait

Wilderness Road
https://en.wikipedia.org/wiki/Wilderness_Road

Defence of Fort M'Henry, Frances Scott Key;
Library of Congress, 17 September 1814

Alleghany-Elliston-Ironto-Shawsville, LINC Letter,
2018, p 1 lincletter.com

"The Legend of Christina Crewey," article by Bob
Shelton in *Virginia's Montgomery County,* Mary
E. Lindon (Montgomery Museum and Lewis
Miller Regional Art Center, 2009, pp 569-572).

*Library of Congress – The Star and Herald
(Christiansburg, Virginia) 18??-1860*
https://www.loc.gov/item/sn94060204/

*Library of Congress – New Star (Christiansburg,
Va.) 1860-18??*
https://www.loc.gov/item/sn90069181

*Library of Congress – The Weekly Herald
(Christiansburg, Montgomery County, Va.) 1854-
18??* https://www.loc.gov/item/sn98068368/

*Library of Congress – Montgomery News
(Christiansburg, Va.) 1924-1931*
https://www.loc.gov/item//sn88064266/

*Library of Congress – Montgomery News
(Christiansburg, Va.) 1931- 1967*
https://www.loc.gov/item/sn86064267

*Library of Congress – The News Messenger
(Christiansburg, Va.) 1967-1974*
https://www.loc.gov/item/sn95079330

*Library of Congress – The Blacksburg-
Christiansburg News Messenger (Christiansburg-
Blacksburg, Va.) 1974-1978*
https://www.loc.gov/item/sn95079335

Library of Congress – The News Journal (Radford, Va.) 19??-1993
https://www.loc.gov/item/sn98068334/

Since 1869 / News Messenger
https://montcova.com/

Michael Walters, Sr.
https://www.geni.com/people/Michael-Walters-Sr/6000000001970551383

Christiansburg, Virginia Newspapers published in Christiansburg
https://roadsidethoughts.com/va/christiansburg-xx-montgomery-localpapers.htm

The Wayfaring Stranger (song)
https://en.wikipedia.org/wiki/The_Wayfaring_Stranger_(song)

The Libby Prison Hymn
https://repository.library.brown.edu/studio/item/bdr:278571/

The Walters Cemetery
http://files.usgwarchives.net/va/montgomery/cemeteries/walters.txt

Photos

Hograth's *Noon*, from Four Times of the Day, 1738 Carving, St. Giles in the Field Church in the background, London, U.K., p19

Account sheet from the slave ship Molly. Royal Museums, Greenwich. The Collection https://collections.rmg.co.uk/archive/objects/466064.html

Gardens and Governor's Palace, Colonial Williamsburg, Francis Benjamin Johnson, Wikimedia Commons

Conestoga wagon or prairie schooner, Pearson Scott Foresman, Wikimedia Commons

Fry-Jefferson Map, 1752, Josiah Fry & Peter Jefferson

Reconstruction of 18th century bottle type brick kiln, Colonial Brickyards, Historic Camden https://www.cityofcamden.org

Settlers clearing land a-logging-bee-in-muskoka-e1526822029467.gif

General Andrew H. Lewis, Find-A-Grave,
https://www.findagrave.com/memorial/886293
1/ andrew-h-lewis

French Indian War, Felix Carrabout-1870

Dr. examining child for smallpox during
epidemic of 1759,
https://www.facebook.com/Winchester-Tales-
111381873717547/photos/pcb.1454890036401
67/145487726973628

Pioneer Smokehouse, Smokey Mountains,
https://Pinterst.com

Lattimer's Old Mill, Post card, 1906

Mason and Dixon Surveying the Line, Artist
unknown, *The Leading Facts of American
History,* p 92; D. H. Montgomery, Ginn & Co.,
New York, NY, 1910

Farming in Colonial Virginia, Virginia Colony
Demographics https://sites.google.com

Augusta County, November 12, 1738,
eWV Encyclopedia

Fincastle County, Virginia, 1732—1738,
Historical Society of Western Virginia, Roanoke,
Virginia

Kentucky County Virginia, en.Wickidedia.org

Carpenters Hall, Philadelphia, postcard, K.F. Lutz, 1949, Freelibrary.org

Divisions of Fincastle County, 1776, Kentucky Secretary of State, Geographic Materials, http://www.virginiapalces.org/boundaries/kybo undry.html

Major General Richard Montgomery, 1775, https://e.wikipedia.org

Virginia Gazette, Williamsburg, Virginia, August 25, 1775, allthingsliberty.com

Colonel George Washington, 1772, Wikipedia Commons, Wikipedia.org

Capture at Winchester, Virginia Militia, https://wikiwand.org

Colonel William Preston, https://findagrave.com/photos250/photos/200 3/270/7727

Battle of King's Mountain, https://en.m.wikipedia.org/wiki/Battle_of_King s_ Mountain#

William Campbell (general)
https://en.wikipedia.org/wiki/William_Campbel
l_ (general)

The American Revolution Revisited, *The Economist,* June 29, 2017,
https://www.economist.com

Mary Draper Ingles,
https://www.findagrave.com

Ingles Ferry as it appeared circa 1906. (D. D. Lester Collection, Montgomery Museum & Lewis Miller Regional Art Center)

Washington at Valley Forge, Getty Images, fair use

Captive running the Shawnee gauntlet, Edward Eggleston, Elizabeth Eggleston Seelye; Tecumseh and the Shawnee Prophet, 1 January 1878

Federal Hall, postcard, New York Public Library, Https://www.janos.nyc

President Washington's house in Philadelphia
https://en.wikipedia.org

Colonel William Christian, Montgomery Museum, Christiansburg, VA

Anna Smith Strong, Heather Blanton's Ladies in Defiance,
https://ladiesindefiance.com/tag/anna-smith-strong/

Nancy Hart https://www.sameshield.com

New Hans Meadow Plantation House built in 1849, Montgomery Museum, Christiansburg, Virginia

Lansdowne Portrait
https://en.wikipedia.org/wiki/Lansdowne_portrait

Rosanna, Hiram and Catharine on stage, Virginia Dwarf Family,
https://appetite4history.com/2016/10/05/the-story-of-the-virginia-dwarf-family/

Walters Farm Cemetery
http://www. findagrave.com

Barnum's American Museum - Wikimedia-commons

Thomas Lewis Grave Marker, Alleghany-Elliston-Ironto-Shawsville, LINC Letter, 2018, p 1
http://www.lincletter.com, fair use

Lewis-McHenry Duel Historical Marker
http://www.hmdb.org

Index of Real People

www.ingramcontent.com/pod-product-compliance
Lightning Source LLC
Chambersburg PA
CBHW051536260626
47170CB00003B/958